Repenter: The Hidden Chapters

Players of the Game: Book 1.5
James McGowan

CONTENTS

REPENTER: THE HIDDEN CHAPTERS

Players of the Game: Book 1.5

A Novella by James McGowan

©2014-2020 by James McGowan

Published 2020 by James McGowan

Cover by Mikhail Palamarchuk

Cover Design by Tony McGowan

Maps by Tony McGowan and James McGowan

Website: stelfire.com

Facebook Fan Page: JamesMcGowanAuthor

Join the James McGowan Reader Group at stelfire.com

Get a notification email for all new releases in the series at https://books2read.com/author/james-mcgowan/subscribe/1/174474/

Join the James McGowan Reader Group!

Go to stelfire.com or use the QR code above to join James McGowan's Reader Group to receive the monthly newsletter. Get the latest missives on works in progress, novel and comic book recommendations, video game and movie obsessions, along with character profiles and fantastic artwork.

ACKNOWLEDGMENTS

Special thanks to Victorine Lieske. She gave me a manner of invaluable advice on getting started on the self-publishing journey. Her generosity is deeply appreciated.

DEDICATION

This novella is dedicated to the memory of Mike Cornell. Long ago, he helped me build worlds.

PLAYERS OF THE GAME SERIES

FOREWORD

The events in this anthology novella take place between the early chapters in Repenter. However, these stories can be read either before or after reading the main novel.

TROJISI CALENDAR

The Trojisi year has 389 days, each lasting 24 hours. The following bi-months comprise the calendar:

1) Pyrene: 63 days.

2) Blite: 67 days.

3) Trires: 64 days.

4) Quatres: 65 days.

5) Quintember: 65 days.

6) Hexember: 65 days.

The ambient etherea in Trojis, Sufrinzon, and their related realms extends all mortal life by a factor of six percent.

TROJIS
NORTHWESTERN JEEA

The Holy Alliance and Temple Tavomine loom to the Southeast.

500 Trecs

MUN'LA

Nor'Ocean

Lake Divinity

The
S T R E T C H

● City
of
Divinity

Kri
● Enclave

River of Thorns

*Lake
of
Tears*

*Boiling
Strait*

The
FIRE WELL

Clondy
● Town

*Vol'sa
Rivers*

Bellsu ● ● Ruby
● Beo

*Mad
Lands*

MUN'MOLLA

NEW GRELLAND

*Mad
Lands* *Boiling
Bay*

● Hiver
Town

Mad Lands

CIGARS WITH MOM: REPENTER CHAPTER 0.1

The Dusk Hour of Pyrene 44th, 1511

Jillian Stefire swayed through the crowded café's narrow confines with familiar confidence. Dim lights gleamed upon a few dozen stool-sized tables, though most of the patrons stood and mingled. Most wore dress attire, dresses or suits. A few of them glanced at Jillian's many black tattoos with passing interest before returning to tepid conversations to match their lukewarm beverages.

Ashe sat at a small table in the back of the café. He tightly clutched his steaming red tea in its ceramic cup. The heat calmed him enough to repress enraged shivers, but not enough to stop his racing mind. He hated her, yet here he sat, early for a meeting in one of the Cosm's many social clubs with his mother.

She still wore form-fitting attire, a rose-hued, fiber-mesh, mancer suit. Her fingers brushed through her thick red bangs. A few strands of white drew her son's notice. Time had not stood still for either of them. At forty-six, she was only seventeen years older than his twenty-nine. Ashe released his beverage and gestured to the chair in front of him with what he hoped was a blank expression.

His mother grinned. She pivoted the chair when she reached the table, sitting in it backwards with her elbows draped across its back. She held a cigar in each hand. Jillian placed one cigar in front of Ashe and pointed her finger at the end of the other in her hand. A small flame erupted and immediately extinguished, leaving a red-orange ember. She took in a deep drag and blew it out above their heads. The spicy-sweet scent did not call to mind tobacco. It smelled of autumn, of leaves burning upon cinnamon. Ashe did not take his mother's offering, leaving it untouched in front of him.

Her green eyes never left his. In the silence, more aromatic puffs of smoke wafted from her nostrils and mouth. Jillian sat up straighter, running a hand down her vest. She spoke around her cigar. "You dress in black, like your father."

Ashe took a long sip of tangy and bitter red tea, his grip on the cup unfaltering.

"But you still have my eyes, my hair." She bobbed her eyebrows. "My talent. You're a pyromancer on the rise."

The son looked past his mother, searching for anything, anyone that didn't belong. The press of bodies in the narrow interior limited his surveillance, but nothing appeared amiss.

His eyes returned to her. Jillian stared at him with the cigar now in the center of her lips with smoke fuming from her mouth. She removed it and tapped a few ashes on the floor. "See anything?"

Ashe shook his head.

She rubbed an eye with one of her palms. "I don't expect forgiveness, sweetie. I left you. I knew you could die, and I still did it. I also know you don't care why I did it."

"Wrong," he said.

Her brow furled for a moment. "Dear gods, you sound just like Stahn."

Ashe released his tea cup. "I guess I do. I can't remember Dad that well." He snatched the unlit cigar and examined a red and white snake emblem imprinted on its brown wrapping. "Tell me why you left me, Jill."

He got the reaction he wanted at the use of this mother's first name, an ever-so brief glimmer of hurt in her eyes. It vanished when she took another puff. "Money and power."

"TELL ME WHY!" Ashe shouted it in her face loud enough to interrupt the café's clamor. Many eyes turned in their direction. "Tell me why. Specifically."

She didn't speak. Moments passed while she smoked her cigar with a stern and bitter expression. At last, the din of conversations returned. She spoke in the renewed privacy. "I had a deal with Baron Jonas in Sufrinzon. He offered me the world to come work for him. He wanted you as a blood sacrifice to enhance our power. I left you and told him you ran away. I started working for him after that." She lowered her cigar with a plume of smoke. "Until I stopped."

"He's after you," Ashe said with bitter certainty.

She nodded. "Nothing I can't handle. He doesn't have friends here in the Cosm."

"He can hire someone to find you."

"We'll be gone by then."

Ashe leaned against the round back of his polished wooden chair. He rolled the cigar between his fingers. "Tell me what you want, Jill."

She took her first name in stride this time. "Gaun herbs. These cigars add years to your life after you smoke them. They cost me plenty. Forboda has a stash of pipes sitting in one of their secret vaults. Five-hundred of them. Each worth about five million decalits in Decadia. The pipe's bowls continually regrow the herbs. If you have one, you're set for life. A very long life. I know where the vault is. I need your help to break in."

Ashe ran his cigar along the bottom of his nose, taking in the strong, bitter aroma. He then drank down his red tea in two gulps. Its heat did not scald his tongue and throat. No heat harmed him while he wore his cloak. He placed the cigar in a pocket inside the black vestment. "Thanks for the gift."

"Sweetie, wait." Jillian reached toward him.

He swatted her hand away and stood. "You're a fool and a waste."

His mother pointed her cigar's glowing ember at him. "Don't let anger get in the way of this. We are talking about billions of decalits." Her eyes widened to show a few bloodshot, zig-zagging lines. "Billions."

"Yes, we are." Ashe held up a finger. Fire ignited upon it. "One of two things will happen. Either you'll succeed in raiding a Nagus Queen's treasure trove. And if you do, I'll find you and take the pipes from you by any means necessary."

A second finger joined the first, also alight with a flame. "Or you'll die trying. Then I'll find out the location of this vault and steal the pipes." He closed his fingers into a fist. The fire around his entire hand brightened to a red hue before vanishing. "Either way, I win and you lose."

She tapped her thumb against the back of the chair. "If I'm a waste, what does that make you?"

"Someone who's going to be very rich very soon." He narrowed his eyes. "Count on it."

"I'll break in without you, then." Jillian rose to her feet. "And you're welcome to try to steal the pipes from me." She placed the cigar back in her mouth and blew smoke into his face. "In fact, I dare you."

"I dare a lot, Jill. It's how I thrive." Ashe pulled his cloak's hood over his short red hair. "For what it's worth, I hope you succeed. I very much want to take them from you."

More smoke huffed from her mouth. "You won't."

Ashe turned his back on her and shoved his way through the crowd.

He never saw his mother again. Two days later, a Nagus Queen petrified Jillian Stelfire into stone in Forboda and shattered her body to pieces. When Ashe Stelfire learned of it, he shed no tears.

THE KEY TO A BRIGAND'S HEART: REPENTER CHAPTER 0.2

Corsis meandered next to Ashe Stelfire. The black-clad pyromancer held up his gnarled pipe, examining it in the dim light of the Underguild's Chalding Pavilion. Elaborate, feathered tarps hung from the ceiling, giving the appearance of overhanging plush pillows. Several hundred mancers mingled within it, all recipients of secret invitations to the Gaun Herb Bazaar, the first and last gathering of its kind.

After much prodding a few days earlier, Corsis at last got the pyromancer to reveal what happened thirty-nine years earlier. Ashe said he raided the treasure trove of a Nagus Queen in Forboda and stole a collection of gaun herb pipes. He had kept the pipes all this time, never once attempting to sell them until now. In exchange for half the profits, Corsis arranged for this gathering to distribute the pipes to Underguild members of his choosing. Individuals who could both afford the sizable asking price and appeal to Corsis as interesting sorts.

Ashe ran his thumb over the polished wood of the pipe. "I'm keeping this one. Thought I could part with it, but I can't. I trust you don't have a concern with that."

"Do as you will. I'm most pleased with today's fortunes." Corsis waited for a quartet of women in flowing gowns with polished rubies in place of their eyes to walk past earshot before continuing. "When I sat next to you and Nirva earlier, you seemed distracted, nervous." Corsis reached a scaled hand into his silken jacket's pocket and produced a coin. "I'll give you my lucky silver if you tell me why."

Ashe held up a hand to refuse the bauble. "Your teeth look sharp. And your bodyguard is intense. It's an unnerving combination."

Corsis ran a finger over his crocodilian lower jaw, pricking his forefinger over a few pointed incisors. "I suppose I do look on the scary side. Would you believe that I'm largely a vegetarian?"

Ashe smirked at him.

"It's true. Fruit in particular."

"Fruit." Ashe's eyes remained fixed on him. "Did Nirva send you to talk to me?" Ashe nodded through the bustling crowds of mancers and guild merchants. Corsis followed his gaze to a red-haired woman leaning against a pillar supporting many fluffy tarps. She wore an open, though tightly fitting, red overcoat with boots that extended up to her thighs. A bald man with golden glyph-covered skin loomed next to her, arms crossed with a thoroughly disdained expression. "You left your bodyguard with her. That surprised me. He doesn't like me."

Corsis shrugged. "He dislikes all kinds of people."

Ashe stuffed the pipe in a pocket inside his black cloak. "So you left him with the woman who's trying to extort, seduce, or trick me into participating in a plex hex that will leave her pregnant with my child."

"I thought you two were intimate."

"Intimacy and trust aren't the same thing."

Corsis couldn't have said it better himself, but he wasn't about to admit that. "I'm not here to convince you one way or the other on Nirva's proposition. I actually wanted to talk to you about our business."

Ashe raised an eyebrow. "Go on."

"Are you the sort who might donate a portion of the proceeds from the gaun herbs' sales to the Underguild's research labs? We've been looking for a means of reviving victims of petrifaction, even those who were shattered to pieces."

Ashe's eyes narrowed. "You heard what happened to my mother decades ago."

Corsis nodded. "I'm actually surprised that you took this long to sell the pipes from your subsequent raid."

"They were an investment, and it's time to cash out."

"Why?"

"That's my business."

Corsis already knew he planned to fund yet another raid on an ancient forest in Inner Yeom for curative sap. In his trade, he often learned things others thought secret. "And can your business spare any funds for the research I mentioned?"

Ashe gritted his teeth. "Not a penny."

A very long, silent moment passed between them before Corsis at last said, "Well, let me know if you change your mind."

"It won't."

Corsis turned his silver coin between his thumb and forefinger. "I'd say time will tell, but that time is now. And you have convinced me. Perhaps Nirva will find the generosity that you could not."

Ashe merely barked out a laugh.

"If you'll excuse me." Corsis parted company with Ashe, shaking his head. The man was a thug, a glorified mugger, a brigand. And yet, Corsis found himself interested in the pyromancer's potential. This man might make a most entertaining addition to the Game. Time would indeed tell.

A few other invitees spoke a few niceties to the reptilian mancer as he wove his way back to Nirva and his gold-skinned bodyguard, Garland. Nirva gestured with a broad sweep of her arm. A few of the bracelets along her wrist jangled together. "Why isn't anyone in here smoking these pipes?"

"Modesty perhaps." Corsis looked from the ruby-eyed women to a horned man with the left-half of his body engulfed in violet flames that gave off no heat, and then through the throngs of the secret bazaar. None brandished the pipes they had purchased. Only Ashe had done so, and he did not smoke his. "But I'm betting it's something relating to a collective lack of trust."

"That's moronic." She beckoned at him with a pair of fingers. "Give me yours. I'm taking a drag."

Corsis reached into a breast pocket and pulled forth a tin. He opened its spring-loaded top to reveal a toothpick-sized cigarette. "I didn't purchase a pipe, but if you really need to light up, here you go. My last one."

She snatched the cigarette and lit it with the glowing tip of her finger. "Last one? I don't buy that." She sucked in the smoke and blew it upward into Garland's face, who made no reaction. "You just don't have them with you."

REPENTER: THE HIDDEN CHAPTERS   17

Corsis snapped the tin shut, savoring the spicy scent that had made its way to him. "Guilty."

"Get another. Join me."

"Later perhaps." He placed the tin back in his breast pocket. "First, I want to know if you still intend to go through with the plex hex only with Ashe Stelfire and no other candidates. This gathering has plenty of men who would gladly participate. It's why I invited you here. Do you see any alternates?"

A devious grin crept over her face. "It has to be Ashe. His pyromancy. His temperament."

Corsis took in Nirva's stern but comely visage. Inspiration struck. "I have an idea. Ashe hunts treasures. I happen to know one he will no doubt covet."

Nirva took another hit from the diminutive gaun herb cigarette. "And what would that be?"

Corsis leaned in closer to her. "I have Retributor."

She nearly dropped the cigarette from her sagging jaw. "We're talking about the lost adapting blade, right? The weapon crafted by Gathiner, God of Invention?"

Corsis kept his eyes fixed on her. "The same."

Both she and Corsis looked at Ashe. He spoke with one of the ruby-eyed women, appearing distracted and disinterested. "I'll have to bring it up with him later," Nirva said. "Say I found its location from someone else, somewhere else."

"Yes, that would be wise."

"He'll actually go through with it if it gets him closer to Retributor." She sucked down more of the cigarette. "Worried that he'll try to raid it from you?"

"No." Corsis narrowed his eyes in Ashe's unknowing direction. "It's quite safe from him. The only way he'll get that weapon is on my terms." He clicked his lengthy jaw shut. "And my terms have bite."

POST-COITAL DESIGN ADVICE: REPENTER CHAPTER 1.1

Two Years Later:
The Late Night of Pyrene 50th, 1551

Ashe leaned against a window of six-inch-thick, opaque glass. He clenched his eyes shut for a moment, fighting a surge of vertigo. Nirva lay in the oval-shaped bed behind him. The plex hex was over. He stared hard at the window, trying in vain to view the exterior of the villa. Dread churned through his insides. His bare feet writhed against the polished, stone-tiled floor. He made a mistake. He already knew it.

"Success." Nirva's dark voice carried no anxiety, only satisfaction. "I'm pregnant."

He didn't bother asking how she knew this soon. Warm air wafted upon his unclothed body from the vents in the ceiling. "Tell me."

"Tell you what?" Her voice carried more than a question.

"You fucking well know what. Where is Retributor?"

She sighed in a hoarse crescendo. "You're in that big of a hurry?"

Ashe tapped the glass with the butt of his hand. "You still want me having no part of this child's life?"

Nirva didn't immediately respond. "It would be best if you didn't. I have plans."

Ashe turned from the window and scowled at her. She made no attempt to cover her nude form. She reclined on the bed with her arms crossed behind her head. The pale light from the window touched her pale body, muting the red brilliance of her hair. It also revealed the painting hanging above the bed. It was one of Nirva's many abstract pieces. This one depicted a series of jagged, red brushstrokes on a yellow background. Not for the first time, Ashe wondered if Nirva's skill as an artist influenced his decision to enter this deal. "What plans?"

"Personal ones." Her expression soured. "You know what? You're right. You should leave." The nude woman sat up, knees close to her chest. "Retributor is in Corsis's possession. Probably in his lair, but that's uncertain."

Ashe's stomach sank. Corsis was on a very short list of people whom he dared not cross. The bipedal, reptilian man possessed riches beyond reckoning, but power to match it. The pyromancer swallowed hard. "Lovely."

She ran her hand down the length of her bent leg. "I never said you'd like my answer.

His eyes locked with hers. The passion from every previous encounter no longer showed within them, only cold contentment.

"The look on your face is by far the best thing to come out of this." A smile retook Nirva's face. "And a lot of good things came out of this."

Ashe's muscles tensed. "Yes, quite a few." The urge to do something violent clattered at the back of his mind. He did not act on it. This woman now carried his child. She also outmatched him. Despite her deception, Ashe knew this plex hex imbued her with added might. The risk was worth it to learn Retributor's whereabouts. He now stood closer to that goal.

He approached his discarded clothing, intermingled with hers in a trail from the suite's door to the bed. Ashe redressed within a minute, hurriedly pulling on his hooded cloak and fastening his bandoliers.

Nirva remained on the bed, watching him like a predator, a gorgeous predator. She offered no further words.

Ashe reached in one of his cloak's inner pockets and pulled out an old cigar held within a white suede sleeve. The soft cloth's preservation hex kept it from deteriorating. He bought the sleeve soon after his mother died, intending to save it for the right moment. And this was it. The pyromancer gently removed the cigar, exposing it to the air.

Nirva frowned at it. "I thought you just smoked that ugly pipe."

"Special occasion." He touched the brown tip with a flaming finger, lighting it. Succeeding where his mother failed, Ashe raided the Nagus Queen's vault and sold the gaun herb pipes. He kept three for himself, one on his person and the other two hidden in different locations. Ashe should have been an old man by now. Instead, he entered his eightieth decade as spry as the day he met with his mother. He sucked in the bitter smoke. Despite his efforts, it lost its rich scent. His pipe tasted so much better.

She gestured to the door. "That smells like a dead rat smoldering in a chimney. Get out."

"In a minute." Ashe lowered the cylindrical roll from his mouth. "What are you planning on naming the baby?"

Nirva stood from the bed, hands on her shapely hips. "No. You don't get to know anything about her."

"I didn't." Ashe returned the awful-tasting cigar to his open-mouthed smile. "But now I know it's a 'her'."

She gestured to the door, and it swung open. "Leave."

He nodded to the yellow and red painting above the bed. "One last thing and I'm gone. It's about your work of art."

"If I have to ask again, I'll impale your testicles on the same skewer as your eyes and eat them in front of you." Nirva pointed at him now, ready to call forth a hex.

"Your painting needs some blue for contrast. I think our child would like that." Ashe departed the suite into the villa's garden maze of thorn bushes.

WEAPONS COVETED: REPENTER CHAPTER 1.2

One Bi-Month Later:
The Morning of Blite 15th, 1551

A little girl wept in Ashe's mind. She would not stop.

"Focus," he said aloud to no one.

Her sobbing, the memory of it still fresh, did not abate.

Ashe sat alone, staring at a red, leather-bound book. He rubbed his eyes, unable to concentrate on its blocky text.

He purchased the tome from the Underguild with the proceeds from a recent raid. The book commanded a staggering price of ten billion decalits, but one he happily paid. It contained the techniques for mastering the Giga-blast hex, one of the most devastating uses of mancy ever devised. Less than a dozen people had ever successfully cast it. Ashe intended to add himself to their number.

First, however, he needed to ensure that the book didn't hide anything that would kill him or spy on him. Ashe didn't trust the Underguild. He needed to scrutinize the book for any traces of malignant mancy or technology. And that meant reviewing it in one of his safe houses far away from his tower in Narath. He looked away from the tome's blocky script at the wooden walls of his safe house's interior. Near the ceiling, a pair of flaming orbs emitted soft light. The sparse furnishings of the desk, chair and the cloth cot were all he needed inside. Outside, a few dozen pyromancy hexes would incinerate anyone who attempted to enter without his consent. He just needed to focus.

Except he could not get the images of the past raid out of his mind. The frantic dash with the red gold from Baron Jonas's treasure trove. The fight to escape. More than anything else, the terrified face of a child he helped free. A little Sphinx who looked like a mix of a four-year-old Human and a lion cub, though she was likely older. He saved her in the chaos.

"Ashe, open the door," a deep voice said from outside the safe house, muffled by the walls. "It's Gnorok. I want to talk. Just talk."

Ashe bolted out of his chair, wand in hand, burning like a welder's torch. He approached the door. "Are you alone?"

"I am."

"How did you find me?"

"Reconnaissance."

Ashe clenched his jaw together. He said the exact same thing to Gnorok a few days ago. Different circumstances, similar anxiety. "I'm opening the door. If you try anything–"

"Yes, yes. You'll hurt me. Your dick is bigger than mine. Just open the door please."

Ashe grabbed the brass doorknob and yanked open the door. Gnorok stood in front of him with arms crossed over his bare chest. He wore a mask of black scarves with his yellow reptilian eyes and the red skin around them exposed. His loose-fitting pants were made of the same material as his scarves. Broad, leathery wings folded at his back. Ashe noted that his visitor's narrow-bladed axe was nowhere to be seen.

The rest of the paved street behind him looked empty, and no activity revealed itself in the other nearby buildings. The city of Drown smelled of mold. A blackened layer of filth lined the edges of its streets. Much of the city bustled with activity, but not this section. This section had been abandoned after a cult of serial killers set up their headquarters in the adjacent building. Ashe had killed all of them long ago, but no one else knew that. Gnorok obviously wasn't afraid to tread here.

The red man looked at the burning wand, then stared hard at Ashe. "You mind putting that thing away?"

The wand extinguished and Ashe lowered it to his side, though he did not put it away. He stepped outside and closed the door behind him, which reactivated the safe house's protective hexes. "Speak your mind."

"I want to know how you knew about my rescue mission for Solneena."

Ashe raised an eyebrow. "That's the little Sphinx's name?"

"Yes. And you were there with your friends, raiding his treasure trove at the same time I staged my attack. That isn't a coincidence. You admitted as much."

Ashe glanced up and down the street, searching for anything amiss. He saw nothing. "Gnor, what can I say? You didn't exactly make it a secret that you were going to attack Jonas City. You marched in the middle of town and all but threatened to do it. Didn't take a lot of effort to determine when you'd be attacking his castle."

"Describe the effort, Ashe."

"I bribed one of the guards to let me know when you attacked."

"So I was your diversion."

Ashe shook his head. "A diversion doesn't save a kid."

"I think it can."

Ashe wanted to tell the winged man that he didn't care. Instead, he said, "Is the Sphinx girl okay?"

Gnorok's head took on a slight tilt. "Traumatized, but alive."

"Her father didn't make it, did he?"

Gnorok shook his head and lowered it, remorse plain in his eyes.

"And her mother is probably angry I had anything to do with the affair."

"Ramansa is angry that we needed your help. It wasn't my finest hour." He refocused his attention on Ashe. Neither spoke. Fighting against Jonas when the pyromancer had already burgled the red gold coin, compelling his partners to rally against the private army, standing between a terrified little girl and the Demon Lord who abducted her. It was not Gnorok's finest hour, but it was Ashe's.

He did it because of the daughter he would never know. Raised by a cold woman in a cold place he could only imagine. He saved the little Sphinx because another parent deserved the chance denied to him. The chance to comfort a scared child.

Gnorok's wings bunched together a little tighter at his back. "Should I tell Ramansa that she owes you a favor?"

Ashe grinned at the winged man. "Let her think that."

"And does that constitute a favor on my part?"

The grin on the pyromancer's face regressed to a thin line. "What do you want, Gnor?"

"There's a weapon you're looking for. If you get it, I want to buy it from you."

Ashe's stomach tightened. He currently searched for more than a dozen rare weapons. One in particular was an adapting blade crafted by a forgotten god. The mother of his unborn child told him of it and the all-too-familiar mancer who possessed it. Did Gnorok know? If so, how? Ashe strained all of his anxiety out of his voice, leaving only cool neutrality. "What weapon?"

Gnorok held each hand's clawed forefingers about a foot apart. "You're looking for a Nuul Wand. You don't need it. You have hexes like the Gigablast you currently learn. I need it."

That surprised Ashe. All his concerns about the adapting blade, Retributor, evaporated. The Nuul Wand possessed the ability to annihilate any matter in a globe of black light. Less than a dozen existed. Countless people searched for them. Ashe knew of a few cold leads, but nothing he deemed worth his time to investigate.

His face apparently betrayed him because Gnorok chuckled. "You must have a lot you don't want me to know about."

"Doubtless." Ashe leaned against the door. "But let's not get sidetracked. You want me to sell you a weapon comparable to an antimatter bomb. A weapon I don't have."

Gnorok's eyes widened within the mask of scarves. "But one day you might."

"And why do you need it?"

"I need something for emergencies. Especially in Sufrinzon. The peace between the baronies will not last."

Ashe stepped away from the door. "I'll think about it."

"Keep me in mind, Ashe. Do what I ask, and you won't just have a favor, you'll have an ally." Gnorok spread his wings, muscles rippling. "A guy like you can always use another on your side." The red-skinned man launched into the air, leaving Ashe to reconsider which weapon he desired more.

THE WET NURSE'S LAMENT: REPENTER CHAPTER 1.3

One Year Later:
The Midnight Hour of Trires 12th, 1552

Svithe strode through the wide hallway of Onno's third highest tower. Grey cloth standards covered the rough stone walls every five feet. Palle's insignia, a solid red teardrop, filled the center of each of them. Cones of dim, white light shone down from circular ceiling lamps in the same interval as the draped crimson tears.

A baby cried somewhere up ahead, her tiny voice full of the discontent unique to people less than four weeks old. No guards stood watch. No one at all bore witness to any part of his journey through the tower's inner network of halls and stairs. This was not coincidental. Svithe's Unnotice hex hid him in plain sight. During his journey, he walked unopposed through heavily defended check points.

The little wails at last ceased. Svithe rounded a final corner and came to a far brighter room with an open metal door. Inside, a shirtless, grey-skinned woman wearing a gossamer skirt carried a little baby bundled in a fuzzy blanket. The infant suckled at her breast, gulping loudly. A crib bereft of toys or mobiles sat in the room's center next to a metal rocking chair. A painting of red slash marks crosscut with blue on a yellow canvas hung on the far wall next to a narrowly-vertical window.

The woman's blank face brightened as Svithe rubbed his thumb against his little finger to pause the Unnotice Hex. "Hello, Cecilia."

"Master Svithe," she said in a soft, distant voice.

"Just Svithe, my good woman." The bandaged man ran a gloved finger down part of the doorjamb. Seeing no dust, he leaned against it. "Have you considered what must be done?"

"Yes." She gently untangled the baby's delicate hand from her platinum blonde hair. "You must get Avril away from her mother." Her face tightened in anguish. A pair of tears ebbed from her glossy-black eyes down her cheeks. "Nirva Silv destroys everything she touches."

"I don't disagree." The bandaged man drummed his fingers on his elbow. Cecilia had been enslaved by Nirva a year earlier, transformed by fleshmancy into a mindless, post-Human hybrid. She had served as a handmaiden during Nirva's pregnancy and a surrogate mother after Avril's birth. Five days ago, Svithe restored Cecilia's mind, granting her only the ability to observe in his absence and complete freedom in his presence. He told her she would determine the baby's fate upon his return. "But you have also no doubt seen her creations as well."

"I've seen the painting that she hides from everyone." Cecilia glanced to the canvas behind the crib. "It's not like this one."

The bandaged man stopped leaning and adjusted his hooded cloak. "Nothing is. Nirva created it. She will do anything to bring forth the vision she perceives within it."

"I brought Avril to her today." Cecilia clutched the suckling baby in her arms. "She has plans. Horrible plans."

Svithe nodded. He paced around the nursery, gazing at the rough surface of the canvas. The blue crosscuts looked fresher. Nirva had apparently added them after its initial completion. He looked at Cecilia from behind and wondered how she'd react if she knew he was the one who sold Nirva the fleshmancy node that transformed her. He dearly wanted to see that reaction, but he decided against it for the child's sake.

After a few more minutes, the child finished nursing. The grey-skinned woman patted her back until she burped. Avril then promptly fell asleep.

Svithe approached the open door. "Come with me."

"No." She extended the bundled infant toward him. "Take her."

Without hesitation, the bandaged man snatched Avril away from Cecilia.

The nursemaid's features bunched up in anguish. "This isn't even my face. Nirva took everything from me." She walked to the window, gazing out into the darkness and the faint light emanating from the next spire. "Why did you give me my mind back? You didn't need my consent. You could have taken Avril any time you wanted."

"I certainly could have." Svithe smiled beneath his mask of gauze. "But where's the fun in that?"

She turned back to him in horror. "You're worse than Nirva."

"No, I'm much better. Just not to you." He nodded toward the open door. "I can't leave you here."

"I'm not going anywhere with you." A new tear ebbed down her face. She crumbled to her knees.

"Do you mean that?"

She took in a quaking breath. "Yes."

"I wish I could say you will be remembered, Cecilia." A glowing, glass-like bo staff flashed into his free hand. He pointed it at her. A white-hot Burning Beam annihilated her into a scorch mark against the wall and the window's borders. A sickly, sweet odor flowed through the air.

The baby stirred in his grasp until he softly tapped the staff against her forehead. Avril fell back into slumber.

Svithe stormed to the doorway. He struck the staff against the floor. Fire erupted along the door's borders. Instead of a hallway, a dark, rain-soaked forest loomed beyond its threshold. The staff vanished. He retrieved a folded envelope with Nirva's name written on it from a cloak pocket and tossed it on the floor.

Svithe covered Avril with his cloak and stepped through the Charred Door into the rain forest in the realm of Trojis. The portal slid shut, leaving behind the nursery and the infant's sadistic mother.

The bandaged man left behind a three-word, typewritten note that read, "Your child lives."

ABSENT SUPPLY: REPENTER CHAPTER 4.1

Svithe sat before an unhappy couple inside a subterranean bunker deep within Mount Onno. Light from a few torches flickered in each corner. A musky scent clung to the moistened walls. While dilapidated, this forgotten refuge was secret, and that trumped any consideration of a more comfortable venue with this hateful duo.

The male Demon and Human female indeed despised each other, but also very much needed each other. Enough to plow into a loveless marriage already arranged a few years from now. Nirva Silv needed a nation to wage her war to reunify Sufrinzon. Quar Iniv said he needed her vast power, but Svithe knew that to be incorrect. Many were more powerful than this Human female, but none had her drive, the desire to unite a divided land whether or not its people wanted it. Svithe folded his gloved hands in front of him atop a splintery table of rotting wood, staring at them through his mask of bandages. These two held great potential.

Nirva tapped the tabletop with an impatient cadence. "Well?"

Svithe waited a few moments before answering. "Forgive the delay. Lost in contemplation." He really just wanted to irritate them. "But I have a solution for you. A weapon that has killed trillions in another realm. One I didn't immediately consider." Svithe actually had it in mind for some time. "Ever heard of the A Pox?"

Nirva frowned. "No."

Quar leaned back, his mouth sour. "I haven't either. Why's that? If it's that bad, everyone should have heard of it."

"It happened ages ago in another realm." He paused for effect. A drip of dingy water echoed in the corner in the silence. Svithe continued in a hushed voice. "Very few survived to tell the tale. Even fewer wrote of it. History forgot it."

Nirva stared at him, eyes hard. "But you didn't."

"I make it my business to remember, my dear."

She shared a glance with Quar before turning her attention back to Svithe. "Ok. We're interested. How much?"

"Its price isn't fixed. I need to obtain it first. Then we can discuss compensation."

The eyeless Sokenti Demon's cheek twitched in apparent irritation. "And if we tell you to fuck off and die?"

Svithe pressed his gloved-fingertips against the table. "Then I sell it to someone else. Maybe someone you know. Maybe someone you don't."

Quar shot to his feet. "Is that a threat?"

Svithe made a mental note of Quar's insecurity, something to exploit at another time. He kept his response cool. "No, it's economics. If you don't want my supply, then I'll go where there's demand."

"You don't have it," Nirva said, a barest hint of a smile on her lips. "There is no supply."

"I will. Don't bet against me on that."

Nirva let out a sigh. "Find it and we'll talk more."

Svithe leaned closer. "But I have a second item to discuss."

Quar sat back down, his face weary. "Out with it."

Svithe brought his fingers down to the table, conjuring a hex. A holographic image of a blonde man in white leather armor with a blindfold flickered before them. "This is your cousin, Jasphir Iniv, yes?"

Quar's body stiffened, saying nothing, waiting for him to say more.

The image of Jasphir vanished with a sweep of Svithe's hand. "Your kinsman abdicated his claim to the Barony when he teamed up with Ashe Stelfire."

Nirva balled her hand into a trembling fist at the mention of her former lover.

Svithe continued without acknowledging her discomfort. "However, Jasphir is a threat to your rule, is he not?"

Quar only nodded.

"I have a means to draw him out. Expose him to you."

The eyeless Demon grunted. "What's the catch?"

"Two. It may take a while before I can entrap him. He's extremely cautious. Expect it to take a year or more. And I want you to keep me and my bodyguard on retainer. We can greatly assist you both in your ambitions."

"Who's the bodyguard?" Nirva asked.

"You've met him before." Svithe leaned an elbow on the table. "Garland. He's on loan to me from our mutual acquaintance."

"The sour Rune Warrior?"

"The same." He loosely interlocked his fingers. "So do we have a deal?"

"Deal," Quar said without a glance to Nirva.

The smirk she leveled at her significant other shifted into a toothy grimace when she met eyes with Svithe. "And what of Ashe Stelfire? Does this plan include him?"

"It can. However, I make no guarantees. Ashe is unpredictable and exceedingly crafty."

"He stole my daughter. You will catch him and bring him to me."

She still thought Ashe had kidnapped her infant child years ago. She was wrong. Svithe did it. Her hatred of Ashe made her irrational, easier to manipulate, so he made no effort to correct her. "I will try. As I said, Ashe is a far different adversary than Jasphir."

"Then concentrate on my cousin first," Quar said. A few bloody tears rolled out of his perpetually suppurating eye sockets. "We need him out of the way, Nirva. Your old boyfriend might have to come later."

Nirva licked her bottom lip. "As long as his time comes."

"It shall." Svithe folded his hands together. "All aligned against you shall meet their fates."

GENTLE QUESTIONS: REPENTER CHAPTER 7.1

Two Years Later:
Pyrene 18th, 1570

"Ok, so I got a question."

Gnorok glared at the toddler-sized Imp, a tan-hued Demon with fluttering leathery wings. Their shadow flickered against the cliff face of the butte a few feet away. "Is it an actual question, Thebes, or you being an idiot?"

"Hey!" Thebes raised his yellow goggles to his brow from his sharp, reptilian eyes. "I just think everyone needs to have all their cards on the table." He pointed one of his stubby clawed fingers in Ashe's direction. "Namely, how did Mr. Fire Fucker get here at the same time we did?"

Red flame flared around Ashe's right hand, making Ashe's shadow waver upon the ground's slabs of rock. "Call me that again, and I burn out your tongue."

"Yeah, whatever, Mr.–"

"Shut it!" Gnorok swatted Thebes with a backhanded slap, knocking the Imp several feet back. "One more word, and I halve your commission."

Thebes rubbed the side of his face with a sour expression. He then made a zipping motion along his angular muzzle and kept quiet.

Gnorok turned his attention back to Ashe, staring hard at him from his mask of scarves. "Tell your partners to come out."

Ashe looked around, gazing to the horizon with dingy clouds in the sky and an unbroken plane of rock. He looked at the butte soaring a few thousand feet upward. No others made themselves apparent. "Did they follow me too?"

Gnorok growled out a sigh. "Quit being a jackass."

"They aren't here." Jasphir Iniv and Nunanker, the partners of whom Gnorok fretted, actually vacationed in another realm. Ashe had no intention of sharing the spoils of this raid with his partners.

"If they jump out later–"

"They won't. It's just me, Gnor."

"Okay, then. Let's talk about you." The winged red man took a step toward Ashe. "I know you shadowed Thebes's recon. You want to know where Braulings hid the Nuul Wand."

Ashe's hand remained on fire. "I won't insult you by denying it."

"Good. Normally, I'd be angry about this." Gnorok's shoulders slouched in apparent fatigue. "This isn't normally."

Ashe raised an eyebrow. "Continue."

"You can have the blessed wand. I need something else. I need him to confirm something else. It's about another weapon. One my family is responsible for."

"I'm not getting distracted by another prize, Gnor." The fire on Ashe's hand brightened. "The Nuul Wand. I'm taking it."

"Dear gods, listen to me, Ashe! I am not playing you. I said you can have it. I've got other things on my mind. Bad things that you certainly won't care to hear." He jabbed his thumb at Thebes. "It's why I subcontracted this gentleman for recon. Say what you will about him, but neither of us would be here if not for his talent."

Thebes's expression brightened at that, but he still said nothing. He appeared to heed Gnorok's threat of diminished payment.

Ashe took in the prisoner before them, frozen within a Static Air hex, knelt on the ground. A drop of sweat glistened on the tip of his black goatee. His pointed horns and cloven feet made him a Satyr. Gnorok's body language remained tense. His eyes held their usual steely resolve, but worry creased their sides. Ashe had never seen Gnorok worried before.

The fire on the pyromancer's hand extinguished. He gestured to the motionless Satyr. "Ok. So. How do we deal with the arms dealer?"

"We scare him. You and me. Make him talk. Threaten him."

Ashe raised his eyebrows. "It's my experience that you have to follow through on threats in situations like this."

The winged man leaned in closer. "Then you aren't doing it right. Just follow my lead and we'll both get what we want from Mr. Braulings."

Ashe extended his once-burning hand. "You're the master. Lead on."

The duo shifted their attention to the Satyr in the Static Air field, Braulings. Ashe pulled out his wand. Its tip burned far brighter than the flames had burned upon Ashe's hand. The air around the prisoner wavered. Burning Bonds, chains composed of fire, flared around Braulings's legs and arms, shackling them together. He raised his horned head. He looked from Ashe to Gnorok to Thebes, then let out a sigh. "Stelfire. Son of a bitch. What do you want?"

Gnorok pulled out a narrow-bladed axe that he carried in a loose knot at his side. "First, let's talk about what I want. I want to let you go. Mr. Stelfire wants to burn you alive with the chains that bind you, the ones that aren't even singeing you right now. That will end when he gets mad. Fire will consume you. Parts of you anyway. The good ones."

He lunged at Braulings and plunged his axe's blade into the rock-hard ground, a hair's breadth away from his leg, slicing his filth-covered pants. Gnorok crouched in front of the arms dealer. "If you give me any reason to agree with this pyromancer."

The winged man clutched Braulings's chin, squeezing hard with black-clawed fingers. "This realms-renowned, cruel pyromancer. I'm going to let him burn you after I cut out other parts of my own. The bad ones." Gnorok shoved him on his back. He landed with a haggard grunt. "Will you talk or will you scream?"

He grunted again and hunched up on his elbows. "Talk," he said in a voice full of weariness rather than fear. "Save the threats. I know how this goes."

Gnorok stood up and pulled the axe out of the rock. "You spoke with Svithe recently. You helped him get a mobile sterile room, atomically sealed. Used for containing germ weapons. Was it obtained for an item stolen from Trojis?"

Sweat beaded down Braulings's forehead. "I don't–"

Gnorok grabbed his throat. "Don't say don't."

The Satyr nodded feverishly.

The red-skinned mercenary released his hold. "Now. You were saying?"

Braulings gasped and massaged his trachea. "I was saying that he didn't mention it, but he made no denial when I asked about the rumors of a raided vial of a Trojisi disease."

Gnorok's arm stiffened. One of his yellow reptilian eyes twitched. "Tell me how you heard these rumors."

"Speculation from the Info Company news reports coupled with third-hand accounts from Grellish soldiers who fought in the latest battle against Dread Corps."

Ashe drew in closer. He knew of Dread Corps's decades-long war on Trojis, including New Grelland. However, the last known fight occurred several bi-months earlier in a lengthy isthmus called the Stretch. The Grells were involved, as was another faction, the Krians.

Gnorok supplied some additional information. "It's not a Trojisi disease. It came from elsewhere."

"Oh?" Braulings shifted his weight from one elbow to the other. "Do tell."

"No." Gnorok jabbed a thumb at Ashe. "Tell him where you hid the Nuul Wand."

Braulings let out a ragged laugh. "Fucking sold me out. I'm an idiot."

"No argument," Ashe said. "Who sold you out?"

"Who do you think, Stelfire?" The Satyr coughed with a rattle of phlegm. "Svithe. I bought the fucking thing off him at a discount. And now I find myself here."

Ashe learned of Braulings's purchase of the Nuul Wand through a contact from the Underguild, a secretive organization to which he belonged. It was possible Svithe was the source, but in the end he didn't care. He wanted the weapon. Aloud, he said, "Think what you want. Where is it?"

The arms dealer grinned. "My safety deposit box at the Loci Bank main branch in Gire Town. They won't let you take it without me there, and you know their security. A raid won't work. You should know. You have a box there yourself."

Ashe kept his surprise hidden. The satyr couldn't have known that Thebes and Gnorok would waylay him. That meant that he ferreted out Ashe's account information in advance for other purposes. And if Braulings knew, others did too.

Gnorok glanced at Ashe. "Got what I needed. Want to make a withdrawal?"

"You're offering to help?" Ashe tilted his head. "Why?"

The red man bobbed his blonde eyebrows at the pyromancer. "Because then you'll owe me a favor."

Ashe stood outside the Loci Bank Tower, a cylindrical, glassy skyscraper that brushed Sufrinzon's perpetual ceiling of orange and black clouds. The rest of Gire Town appeared squat compared to the central building. The entire city encircled the bank headquarters in a spiraling pattern, like a billowing cyclone of concrete, glass, and metal. The pyromancer crossed his arms and leaned a shoulder against the red brick wall of a breakfast cafe that served food smelling of pork. Ashe made it a point never to eat such food in Sufrinzon, as it was usually from a sapient being. His mouth did water, however. Not out of hunger, but desire for a long sought-after prize.

Braulings emerged from the tower's revolving doors. Thebes and Gnorok flanked him. The tense trio made their way through the bustling pedestrian traffic of the plaza that the restaurant bordered. The arms dealer clutched a narrow, metal box. Their ruse of the two mercenaries serving as bodyguards apparently worked. That made things considerably easier than plan B. It involved lots of fire. Ashe licked the back of his teeth, ready to unleash a Flame of Tumult if Braulings made any hint of a hostile move. Of course, Gnorok would probably lop off his head before Ashe even reacted.

Thebes darted next to Ashe when they got closer. "That place is crazy nice. The bathrooms have mints." He produced a chalky, soft mint and popped it in his sharp-toothed mouth with a crunch. "Mints!"

Ashe very much wished Gnorok's prohibition on the Imp's talking had lasted longer than a day.

Braulings shoved the box at Ashe. "Take it and piss off."

"Nah, he definitely pisses on," Thebes said.

Ashe barked out a laugh despite his desire to not encourage Thebes. He grabbed the box, popped a pair of latches on the side. Inside, he found a black and white baton with a large button atop it, the Nuul Wand. The pyromancer shut the box. He nodded to Gnorok.

The red man pulled out a black, metal cube the size of a thumb tip and tossed it to Braulings. "Your blotter." He then handed him a folded piece of paper. "And the coordinates to the other data cube containing your client and supplier lists. It's not in Sufrinzon. You'd be wise to never return to this realm."

Braulings glanced over the coordinates before shoving the paper slip in his pocket. "Are we done here?"

Gnorok extended his hand down the street. "Go in peace."

The Satyr took a few steps before turning around. "Sufrinzon is going to collapse in on itself. The baronies will bleed each other dry in the coming war. I hope you all get to watch everything go to shit around you."

"You should have used the bathroom if you gotta shit." Thebes pointed at the tower. "Like I said. Mints."

Braulings glowered at the Imp. He then walked away, merging with the crowded plaza.

Ashe placed the box beneath his arm. "Did the Loci Bank know what this weapon can do?"

"Didn't appear to," Gnorok said.

"Good. I need to go back in there and empty the important things from my deposit box. The security is compromised. You two will find your payment from me in your accounts soon."

"You didn't hire us."

"I'm paying back your favor."

Gnorok chuckled with a devious crescendo. "Doesn't work that way. I'll call in the favor someday. Not today."

"You're a bastard, Gnor."

"The bastardest."

Ashe parted ways with the two winged mercenaries, heading toward the bank tower. He wore a crooked grin. He did have the Nuul Wand after all. That was worth a favor. Hopefully.

PREGNANT WOMEN'S PREFERENCE: REPENTER CHAPTER 8.1

Three Years Later:
Quintember 5th, 1573

Avril Enzali crossed ankles on her comatose father's dust-covered desk. A 2-D rectangular hologram, a screen without a monitor, displayed old footage of her in unarmed combat against a pair of muscular women. One stood a few inches taller with almond-shaped blue eyes and paler skin. Pointed ears poked through her short, platinum blonde hair. The other stood at Avril's height with deep-olive skin, dark, fiery eyes, and a mane of curled black hair. The two women and Avril wore identical loose-fitting, silken tops and slacks that allowed for ease of movement.

The shorter of the women, Kindra Shalai, sent a spinning kick at Avril's face. Her braided red hair lashed back as she dodged Kindra's foot and its laced sandal. The woman with the pointed ears, Een of Muné, jabbed at her throat with an elbow, which Avril also dodged with a nimble spring backward. Kindra anticipated this and intercepted her with a punch to the diaphragm. Avril collapsed to the cement floor of the enclave's sparring room, gasping for breath in a fetal position.

Kindra looked down at her with a face showing a perverse mix of sadism and concern. "You must be better, Krian. Get up."

Avril tapped the lower edge of the hologram, pausing it. She rubbed the center of her chest. This footage was three years old, and the wound had long since healed, but it still hurt when she watched her old sparring sessions with her mentors. Kindra always called her 'Krian' as an insult. The war had decimated Avril's order. Kindra and Een agreed to train her further in the art of combat.

And they did so with avid glee. She considered selecting later recordings of their bladed sessions, but her current mood called for punching, rather than slicing.

She reviewed hours of footage, fast forwarding and pausing, watching her slight improvements in technique as the weeks and bi-months progressed. Een swayed as she fought, moving like a whip. Kindra was far more direct, more akin to a saber. Avril paused the recording again as her past self slammed Kindra against the floor while thrusting her heel into Een's jaw. She knocked both of them out with that move. That triumph still made her grin.

"How often do you watch that one, Avril," Kindra asked from behind. "Once a day? Twice?"

"This is the first time in a while." Avril rose and turned to her visitors, Een and Kindra in the flesh. She had killed the time watching the old footage while awaiting their arrival at the Kri Enclave. However, neither would spar with her today. Pregnancy rounded both women's abdomens. That took Avril aback. Her jaw sagged. "I'd ask what happened, but that's a stupid question."

"Not with Een, it isn't." Kindra rubbed her belly with an absent brush of her hand. The raven-haired woman wore a robe with a gown beneath it.

The edge of Avril's mouth raised in a crooked grin. "What? Did Vick knock both of you up?"

Een flushed while Kindra gave Avril a chilly stare.

The young Krian just shrugged. "Okay, that was out of line." Avril internally added, *"But you both love him and it's fucking obvious."* Aloud, she said, "So what's different about your pregnancy, Een?"

The pointed-eared woman regained her composure. "I swam in a Divinity Pool. I thought you'd remember that about the Chan'la."

Avril did remember that Een's people, an order of warrior women, were said to reproduce without sex, or at least as an alternative means to sex. Avril chose not to believe it. It made her question why the Krians could not replenish their ranks in the same manner. It made her despair. She pushed it out of her mind until now. "Well, awkwardness aside, congratulations to you both."

"You should have led with that," Kindra said, still giving Avril a frosty glare.

Avril met it with steel in her voice. "You know me. Disciple of darkness and all that."

Kindra stayed quiet for another moment. At last, her face softened a bit. "We wanted to let you know that we'll no longer be mothering you." She placed both hands along the sides of her belly. "Others will require that attention."

"This fledgling left the nest long ago." In truth, Avril's tutelage had ended a year earlier on their last visit. They had little else to teach her in a training environment. Avril now learned in the field, constantly striving to improve on her quest to free her imprisoned goddess from the Holy Alliance. The education nearly killed her on several occasions.

Een sauntered next to Avril. The taller woman leaned upon the desk, looking at the still playing images of their old sparring matches. "You're better now, but not the best."

Avril rapped her hand on the desk. "I'm hardened. I'll perfect my art. Believe it."

"You don't have to do it alone." Kindra moved her hand toward Avril's shoulder, but then dropped it. "Despite your efforts to anger us, the offer still stands."

"I thought you said you were done mothering." Avril stalked away from the desk and faced both of them, irked but not surprised. "You were both there when the War of No Hope ended. You saw my order decimated. You could have helped us rebuild and recruit." Her eyes widened. "But you left us to decay. Only four of us remain, and one of those is my comatose father. The man my goddess can help. But you won't help me."

"We'll help you," Kindra said in a low, calm tone.

"If I forsake my faith. That isn't help. That's extortion."

Een crossed her arms. "You know our stance. Celsis Kri, your goddess, led an army that killed our peoples by the hundreds of thousands. New Grelland and Mun'la could have stopped the Eruption and saved the millions that followed. We will not risk starting yet another war to free this woman."

Avril bit the inside of her lip, swallowing back her angry response. Raw emotion never worked with these two. She straightened up her posture, steadying herself. Een could have said something about letting Celsis Kri rot in a much-deserved fate, could have called her evil, an agent of genocide, and she did not. That meant something. It had to.

A deep weariness crept up on Avril. All that she had done since the War of No Hope's end, all the enemies made, all the killing, and still she was no closer to helping her father emerge from his unnatural coma, to freeing the matriarch she had never met. Her order, the Krians, truly could use help. That hard fact hurt. "Is there anything I can do other than deny my goddess?"

Kindra took on an expression of somber fondness. "You may do many things besides that. But we won't give you further support without doing that. Try to understand, child." Kindra put a knuckle to her lips, her face tense, fighting back tears.

After a few more seconds, she lowered her hand and swallowed. "For you, the Eruption is ancient, something that happened dozens of lifetimes in the past. A part of history. Een and I lived it. In our nightmares, we still see the faces of the dead, the land's devastation. Celsis Kri personally killed many of our friends. We won't," she bunched her lips tightly together, then continued, "we can't help her after what she did."

Avril knew this, but Kindra had never explained it with such compassion before. The Krian paced to the other side of the room, putting distance between her and her mentors. All she had to do was say yes. She didn't have to renounce Celsis Kri in her heart. "I can't do it. My father raised me as a Krian. It's who I am." Avril ambled along the wall, gliding her hand over its rough concrete. "With or without your help, I will never stop. I will free her."

"Then it will be without." Kindra then glanced to Een, who gave a solemn nod.

The Chan'la woman strode toward the open door. "Good journeys to you, Avril Enzali." She exited with her robe flowing behind her.

"I didn't want it to end this way," Kindra said, her voice barely audible.

Avril extended her hand toward the door, bidding her to follow Een. "But you had to expect it."

"I did. Be safe, child." Kindra departed, brushing her fingertips along Avril's shoulder as she did.

The Krian watched the pregnant women stride down the hallway. They never gazed back over their shoulders at her. She wished they had.

MEN OF MIST AND METAL: REPENTER CHAPTER 11.1

Two Years Later:
Quatres 45th, 1575

Gnorok dove into the rust-hued snow as the electric surge erupted from the bottom of the hill. The diluted acid within the chilled flakes hissed upon his durable, red skin. He pressed himself against the hill's zenith. The chilled air fell still. A hundred feet below, five metal-clad cyborgs lay sprawled in a circle around a vaguely humanoid shape composed of billowing mist. The fight lasted less than ten seconds. Gnorok didn't relax just yet. These Antagonist Series cyborgs were known to regenerate after seemingly dying, stronger than before.

The spectral man, Arwith, looked up to Gnorok with ice-blue, very Human eyes. His soft-spoken voice sounded in Gnorok's mind via his psionic link. "They're down." He jerked his head down at one of the fallen Antagonists, a grey one with a dark-slotted visor. "Ok, that's a little off."

Gnorok tensed, ready to lunge into the air with his leathery wings. He looked over the expanse of the other hills topped with the same dingy snow, stretching on to the vast mountains in the east. He saw nothing. They were alone.

Arwith held up a frothing hand. "It's fine. It's fine. Just something unexpected. One-in-a-million."

Arwith was a Psyspecter, a living ghost, a mind without a body. The last known manifestation of such a powerful entity occurred centuries earlier. That made Arwith far more rare than one-in-a-million. Gnorok grinned at him from beneath his mask of scarves. "So you're statistician too."

"Ha. No, that's actually another guy from my hometown. A couple, now that I think of it."

The winged man didn't doubt that. Arwith hailed from a city of scholars on Trojis before Gnorok recruited him. "So what happened?"

"I didn't kill this one. For lack of a better term, the electrokinesis rebooted his mind. He's not necessarily hostile anymore."

"Not necessarily." The winged man grasped a handful of acidic snow. It sizzled in his hand as it melted. The sparse precipitation in Sufrinzon seldom took the form of water in any of its states. Much more often it came as cauv, the corrosive liquid that passed for fresh water here. Gnorok stood up. "Can he talk? Is he functional?"

"Yes to both. I'm talking to him now on a different psi-thread. Figured it'd be best to limit the voices in his head."

"I'm coming down." Gnorok spread his wings and soared down to the carnage. He sucked in a frigid breath. Sufrinzon's usual stench of sulfur was muted here, making the air borderline-fresh. The rushing sensation beneath his wings never ceased to exhilarate him. He didn't know how people without wings could stand not being able to fly. He landed amidst the other fallen Antagonists. Their sleek, chrome armor completely encased them with mirror-like visors. They contrasted the survivor's armor's far simpler design, grey and cylindrical, with a black visor. The alloy on this one looked flimsy, like tin.

The red man held his axe at his side, ready to use it, but he hoped he wouldn't need it. "I'm Gnorok, Son of Quoth. Arwith says you can talk. Please tell me your name."

The cyborg's helm swiveled toward the winged man. His voice sounded hollow, synthetic. "Don't remember."

Gnorok decided to extend this metal soldier a sliver of trust, and crouched before him. "What do you remember?"

"Enslaved by Dread Corps. Made me... this." He held up a gauntlet before his dark visor. "Took away everything I was."

Gnorok shared a quick glance with Arwith. The spectral man nodded. "He's telling the truth. It's radiating out of his mind like a fire."

"Any idea why you look different from the other Antagonists?" Gnorok asked.

The soldier paused. "Display in my helmet says I'm older than them. Lots older."

Gnorok stuck the tip of his axe in the snow and sat next to the soldier. He set his eyes on the orange and black clouds beyond the hilltops to the mountains, half-obscured by the miasma. "I've found in life that it's better to first ask others what they want, rather than tell them what I want. So, what do you want, tin skin?"

"Heh. A rhyme. I like that." The soldier's black visor fixed on Gnorok's masked face. "I want to find myself. I want Dread Corps to hurt for what they did to me." He fell silent for a moment. "What do you want?"

Gnorok decided it best to keep his specific goal of reclaiming a stolen vial containing a horrific disease secret for the time being. "I want Sufrinzon weak. A strong land of the damned makes for dangerous times. The Palle Barony colludes with Dread Corps, bolstering that strength. I mean to end that, among other things." He extended his hand toward the soldier. "Do you want to help?"

The cyborg immediately grasped Gnorok's hand in a brief, but firm shake. "Yes. And that name. Keep calling me that."

Gnorok stood up. "Glad to know you, Tin Skin."

THE GOOD NEIGHBOR: REPENTER CHAPTER 11.2

Two Bi-Months Later:
Quintember 60th, 1575

"Oh, Stelfire. Stelfire." Braulings's voice mockingly sang from on the stagnant breeze. "I've come to collect my Nuul Wand. With interest." The Satyr rode upon an iron crown of a misshapen Humanoid brute that looked like someone had doused it in acid. Its slimy flesh hung from its bones. A single bulbous, black eye pulsed with light in the center of its head. Ashe had no idea what it was, so Braulings had his admiration for that.

Ashe leaned atop one of the glossy, black ramparts of his tower. The repulsive giant lumbered toward the structure over an empty field of dead grass, leaving slimy, pitted footprints in its wake. The monstrosity stood the same height as the three-hundred-foot-tall building. The ground visibly shook in its passage, but the tower remained firm. Only a slight tremor reached Ashe's feet. The pyromancer clenched a different wand, his wooden one, in his hand. The Nuul Wand could quickly end this fight, but it also would annihilate the tower. Braulings had to know that.

Ashe considered asking the arms dealer how he found Narath, but it really didn't matter. No words did. The giant's bulging eye fired a titanic bolt of electricity with a deafening rumble of thunder. Its blast stopped a few feet from Ashe, refracting into the sky's murky clouds. The tower's protective hexes held, but they would falter after another few hits like that. The pyromancer stabbed his wand in the giant's direction. A jagged, red Flame of Tumult surged at its misshapen head with Braulings upon it. The blast fizzled like a match tossed into water.

That was bad. The hex drained Ashe's inner reserves. His Flame of Tumult was supposed to incinerate anything it touched. The arms dealer appeared to have expected that. Ashe wouldn't have the strength to cast another hex for at least a minute, time he didn't have. He grabbed for a revolver holstered at his back.

Dark-red light enveloped the towering brute just as Ashe pulled out the handgun. He held his fire. The giant toppled over, gasping for air. It collapsed with a jolting quake, a louder crash that echoed out to the horizon. Ashe braced himself against a rampart to keep his balance in the residual shaking of the ground. Still, the tower suffered no structural damage. He knew this without looking. The building's prior owner built it to withstand far worse than this.

The giant wheezed before making a gurgling noise that regressed to nothing. Braulings rolled off the creature and landed at the feet of a woman encased in ornately crafted plate armor and a helm with horns protruding from the top and the jaw, giving it a vaguely insect-like appearance.

Braulings aimed a wrist-mounted projectile weapon at her. She acted faster. Her two-handed sword plunged into his throat and through the back of his neck. Blood sprayed upon her greaves and the tan grass around him. He collapsed and bled more.

The woman in red armor spoke softly, though Ashe easily heard her from his vantage point. "You're trespassing."

Ashe holstered the resolver and waved to her. This was ViRauni, a Demon hunter who made the eastern forest on the island her home. They had a few dealings in the past, all of them cool but amicable.

She bade him to come down with a slight swipe of her hand.

The pyromancer held up a finger, indicating that he needed a moment. He loosened his tightened muscles at the base of his neck, rocking his head once to the right and then to the left, letting the etherea flow into him again until he had enough for a Levitation hex. With a leap over the black tower's side, Ashe floated down with his black cloak wafting around him. He touched down ten feet away from ViRauni, the dead foes large and small. "You made that fight easy."

She stared at him in silence.

Ashe finally added, "Thanks."

ViRauni nodded. "This fool and his beast plodded through part of my forest. You're lucky they caught my attention."

Ashe opted to keep quiet rather than risk an argument with her over his ability to save himself.

The woman in red armor pointed to Braulings's body. "Do you think he brought others?"

"Hard to say, but I doubt it. I think he spent his resources on the giant. It couldn't have been cheap."

"Tell me the truth. Is Narath safe from further attack? Are your enemies going to make this a habit?"

"Not this enemy." Ashe gestured over the field of dead grass with an out-swept hand. "And I chose this place for its seclusion myself. I don't expect any other visitors."

"Did you expect this one?"

"No." Ashe gave her a sheepish grin. "Between the two of us, we can handle whatever comes our way."

"I won't always notice when trouble comes knocking on your door, Ashe Stelfire."

"And I don't expect you to." He glanced at the dead Satyr's eyes, frozen in hatred and surprise. "But on this occasion, I'm glad you did."

"I strive to be a good neighbor." ViRauni turned from him, walking away from the tower and the death at its borders.

THE END of BOOK 1.5
PLAYERS OF THE GAME

BACK MATTER

BACKGROUND ON THE GAME

In an age long past, two men saved Trojis from the Weird Ones, godlike entities who intended to warp the planet realm to suit their unknowable designs. The conflict is known as the Weird War. One of the men, Corsis, suffered a parting curse by the dying King of the Weird Ones that left him transformed into a bipedal Lizard. The second man, Bennet Burnhelt, was gifted with eternal vitality along with a select few of his elite warriors, while others ascended to godhood. He offered to help Corsis, but the Lizard refused, resentful that he had taken the Weird Ones' parting ire, while Bennet reaped only the benefits of their ruin.

While Bennet rebuilt the world with his immortal allies and the new pantheon, Corsis quested in other realms to reclaim his Humanity and bring the rest of the hiding Weird Ones low. With the Dragon, Quandric, Corsis defeated the Weird Ones, and placed them in a mechmancical (techno-magical) prison in which he siphoned their vast power, becoming a god in his own right. He broke the curse that had made him hideous. He stood triumphant.

But subdued Weird Ones' continued confinement came with a price. They would not stir so long as Corsis continued the Game. Their twisted form of entertainment where they embroiled the realms in perpetual stalemated strife, where no side ever gained the upper hand. Corsis became Master of the Game and it corrupted him all the more. The Weird Ones are no longer a threat, so long as his sadistic cruelty subtly guides the strife of the worlds. History has forgotten Corsis's name. But there are those who know. The Players of the Game. Some who serve him. And others, like Bennet Burnhelt, who stand against him.

Their defiance is made even more difficult by the Rules of the Game, adapted from those of the Weird Ones. Rule 1: To know the name of Corsis is to play the Game. Rule 2: Only Corsis or those working for him can tell someone of the Game's existence. Rule 3: None may seek to harm Corsis or hinder his enjoyment of the Game. Rule 4: Corsis may add or change Rules at his whim.

A fifth Rule exists. One that offers a sliver of hope. One made by Quandric after he parted ways on bad terms with Corsis. The Unsaid Rule. Its details are not known by anyone besides Quandric and Corsis. The Dragon leveraged something against Corsis to force the concession. Other Players know only that enduring trust must be established with those affected by the Game to invoke it. Once this is done, invoking the Unsaid Rule allows them to be filled in without violating the second Rule.

But even with the Unsaid Rule's loophole, breaking the other Rules offers Corsis an excuse to become even more vindictive. To ignite wars of reprisal waged by his surrogates. To inflict personal ruin on those who vex him. But the only way to best him is to break the Rules.

SIGNIFICANT PAST EVENTS OF RELEVANCE

- Year -2500 Pre Eruption: The Weird War is fought. The conflict that started everything in the POTG series. Corsis and Bennet Burnhelt saved the world, but Corsis would come to imperil it.

- Year -15 Pre Eruption: Starm, Balpors, and Celsis Kri start the Holy War.

- Year Zero: The Eruption ignites. Muné is slain. Vurg and Gathiner erect the Outer Wall of the Fire Well. Much of Grelland is shunted to Pendulum, though surviving in New Grelland is aware of this for many centuries as Bennet and Vick strive to save their island from the Fire Well's flames. Starm and Balpors imprison Celsis Kri and start the slow expansion of the Holy War. Darkeyes/Crystala is born to Heathren.

- Year 199: Darkeyes and others have a failed coup against Corsis, which results in an enduring punishment centuries of mental enslavement.

- Year 901: The end of the long sieges of the many Nether Realms on New Grelland with the advent of the mechmancical Locked Doors. Unbreakable constructs of solid energy that resemble sturdy wood, and powered by the Trail Lock power complex in central New Grelland.

- Year 1498: Mary Night's reign of terror in Crystal Keep ends when Xax and the other Buckler's kill her.

- Year 1515: Corsis has Dread Corps start the decades long War of No

Hope after Bennet Burnhelt attempted to tell Starm of the Game.

- 1560s-1570s: Events of Book 1: Repenter and Book 1.5 Repenter: The Hidden Chapters.

.

REALMS

These are dimensions of reality reachable by fifth-dimensional means, like Charred Doors, Dread Doors, Realm Gates, Shadow Shifting, etc. They have an atmosphere and gravity similar to that of Trojis.

Realm Sub-categories:

- Pico Realm: A plane of existence with limited space and finite borders. Inparadis, the Cosm, and the Panic Room are pico realms.

- Planet Realm: A sphere of existence that orbits at least one daystar. Its people are both good and evil. Trojis, Inner Yeom, Outer Yeom, and the Macro Worlds are planet realms.

- Nether Realm: A secluded sphere of existence tainted by evil and peopled by the lost. Despite this, hope does glimmer within them. Sufrinzon, Decadia, and Forboda are nether realms.

- Transition Realms: Places connected to many other realms through physical aspects like lower relative light for the Shade Lands, or mental activity for the Realm of Thought.

Realms of Note:

- Trojis: A wet, blue planet composed of vast oceans and the super-continent of Jeea. It is home to the ceaseless blaze of the Fire Well. The conflicts and culture of Trojis touch dozens of interconnected realms. New Grelland, Mun'la. Crystal Keep, the Union Cities, and the Holy Alliance are counted as its most potent nations. Others like Yintu hide from scrutiny of the greater powers.

- Sufrinzon: A vast Nether Realm often described as a distorted reflection of Trojis. Burning oceans and orange-black clouds encircle it. Despite its darkness, beauty and valor thrive among those who choose freedom over tyranny. It was once divided into several baronies, including Palle, Darbin and Velsuvia. But it has since consolidated into a singular empire, Sufrinzon United, influenced by Corsis from the periphery. Only the remote islands of Narath and Necron remain free.

- The Cosm: The Pico Realm containing the Underguild. A small nation unto itself, the Cosm spans only a city-sized amount of space, yet it has never been fully explored. Its geography shifts over time at the fancy of a select few of its inhabitants.

- The Panic Room: A Pico Realm created by the Sphinx, Ramansa, as a private refuge for her mobile manor. None can gain entry to its churning purple mist without her consent. It can connect to other realms at her direction

- The Shade Lands: The Transition Realm connecting the shadows of all places, people and things. Space is folded within its perpetually twilit environs. If one dares to walk within the Shade Lands, vast distances can be covered in minutes and impossible to reach realms are accessible. However, those who lurk within its dim expanses rarely make such excursions uneventful.

- The Macro Worlds: A network of fifty-five planets all contained within a gas giant's atmosphere of oxygen, nitrogen and carbon dioxide, defying gravity and physics. Trillions of beings once inhabited them. The majority of the Macro Worlds are now lifeless husks after the Underguild ignited their atmosphere to end the A Pox's first pandemic. Little breathable air remains. All of it sterilized.

- Outer Yeom: A desolate planet realm that once rivaled Trojis in cultural influence. Its few remaining people all know the name Corsis and fear it.

- Inner Yeom: A verdant and wild planet realm untouched by the strife of its outer counterpart. The wise forest of Halonir and the Dragon Clan Quandric reside within its plush borders.

- Pendulum: The Pico Realm containing the rest of Grelland, which the gods Vurg and Gathiner shunted from Trojis during the Eruption. It is contested by the surviving Grells and Dread Corps within the confines of its contained semi sphere. Its plight has gone unknown by much of New Grelland and the rest of Jeea.

- Decadia: This entirely urban Nether Realm possesses an advanced capitalistic economy. Its weapons are rivaled only by those of New Grelland and Dread Corps. However, it tends to trade its wares covertly with other nations, rather than overtly enter into conflict with its enemies. The perpetual Old Tempest storm on the opposite side of Trojis permanently overlays Decadia on the island of Lantis and its surrounding waters.

- Forboda: Dominated by the Nagus Demons, humanoids with snake tails in place of legs. Lush rain forests sprawl everywhere. Tales of its subterranean cites' riches have led many a raider to an untimely death.

- The Irrealm: The home realm of the Weird Ones. It is a place of constant flux, where matter and energy are not constant. If its kaleido-scopic madness bleeds into another realm as an Irreal Flare or a Weird One's true form, it distorts the local reality, permanently altering any-thing touched by it. If the effects are contained, it will occasionally leave behind Cataclyse crystals on terrestrial matter. Corsis has a lair within the Irrealm. It has yet to be infiltrated by any of the Players.

- The Realm of Thought: A Transition Realm that intersects with all sentient minds. Astramancers and psionists can project their spirits or consciousness into it. It has two aspects, the Convergence that overlays the reality occupied by a perceiving mind with familiar landmarks and settings. And the Divergence, a pliable area that can change into any environment imagined by those who inhabit it.

- Inparadis: A pico realm created by Starm. It contains two overlapping local realities. One contains his private refuge fortress. The other far larger aspect contains the Dragon Caldera, a mountain-sized pyramid where dire plex hexes are performed and the prisons beneath it of the ice maze and its dungeon annex.

CALENDAR AND MEASUREMENT

Multiple realms, including Sufrinzon, adopted the Trojisi Calendar after the Eruption due to the influence of the Holy Alliance, the Union Cities and New Grelland on inter-realm commerce, politics, and warfare. The calendar is divided in to six bi-months. A bi-month marks the approximate time of 65 days that the moon of Pathine takes to revolve around Trojis.

The Trojisi year has 389 days, each lasting 24 hours. The following bi-months comprise the calendar:

1) Pyrene: 63 days.
2) Blite: 67 days.
3) Trires: 64 days.
4) Quatres: 65 days.
5) Quintember: 65 days.
6) Hexember: 65 days.

The ambient ethereal energy in Trojis, Sufrinzon, and their related realms extends all mortal life by a factor of six percent.

The term "trec" is used in place of mile, and they measure the same approximate distance. Otherwise, imperial measurements such as inch, foot, yard, pound, ton, gallon, etc. are used throughout the text.

Mancy and High Technology

The level of technological innovation in the realms has largely plateaued for thousands of years with a melding of mythic arts, hyper powers, and high technology. Magic is a proven science in this world and is referred to as mancy. It draws on a power source outside of the electromagnetic spectrum called etherea. The mental art of psionics also draws on etherea and the innate life force of the wielder.

Applications of mancy are called hexes. And bigger applications requiring more power and preparation are called plex hexes, short for complex hex. Hex creation requires three components from a mancer:

1) Mental mastery: The mancer must focus all of his or her willpower to conceptualize the hex. Some will perform mental exercises, others will perform physical acts such as subdued verbalization or hand gestures. Regardless of the process, the hex requires mancer's the absolute focus, or it simply fails.

2) Ethereal energy: During their studies, mancers gain the physiological ability to store ethereal energy within their bodies, akin to an electrical battery. Depending on their location, they can allow draw on the ambient ethereal energy of their environment, akin to tapping an electrical line to supplement the power of a battery. Each hex expends ethereal energy. A mancer will replenish the lost energy through food, rest or mancy supplements such as potions and talismans.

3) Triggering Action: Once inner physiology aligns to supply the ethereal energy, and the mind solidifies the concept, a catalyst is required to initiate the hex. A triggering action is most often saying the name of the hex aloud. However, more experienced mancers can create a hex with a mental command. The simpler the hex, the less likely triggering action needs to be spoken.

The more notable fields of mancy specialization include:

- Pyromancy: Fire and heat focused.

- Chronomancy: Temporal distortion focused.

- Mechmancy: Melding of ethereal energy into devices, simple or complex.

- Gunmancy: A subset of mechmancy that focuses on ethereal applications on firearms.

- Necromancy: Focused on the forces of death.

- Aeromancy: Air and electricity based.

- Geomancy: Ground and plant-life focused.

- Hydromancy: Water and Ice oriented.

- Martialmancy: Combat-oriented with an emphasis on speed of creation.

- Fleshmancy: The twisting of biology to create abominations. Kliost flowers are often used to spread it as an infection through airborne particles or in food or narcotic sweeteners.

- Astramancy: Manipulation of the properties of incorporeal realms.

- Alchemancy: The conversion of ethereal energy into matter or the transmutation of existing matter.

- Quandrimancy: The amplification and conversion of different types of electromagnetic or ethereal energy. Named after the Dragon, Quandric, who developed the discipline.

- Mastermancy: The mastery of all forms of mancy. This is limited to beings already possessing immense ethereal energy and centuries of experience.

- Irreality: Not strictly mancy, but a chaotic state of matter and energy constantly in flux. It warps any other forms of matter with which it comes into contact.

- Hrolish: A dark, largely unknown language that can unmake people, attributes, and minds by those who know it.

- Perceptia: A sixth sense that allows insight into thoughts, spirits, and the physical world. It has a Chan'lavian variety that is more acute and limited to Muné and her successors. Wild Perceptia is less acute, but it can be bequeathed to others as either an inherited trait, or passed on at the time of death.

- Al'laan: An innate hyper power of the Chan'la that allows them to manipulate and bend space with varying offensive, defensive, healing, and bio-stasis applications.

Hexes of Note:
- Ashes Away: Scatters detritus from burnt material.

- Ashes to Ashes: Disintegrates victims in a cascading wave.

- Aura of Quandric: Clads a single individual in a second skin of protective force.

- Blood to Boil: Superheats a victim's blood, causing it to bubble out of the orifices of the victim's body.

- Burn: Engulfs a target in fire.

- Burning Beam: Summons a white-hot ray with a potency proportional to its wielder's experience.

- Burst: Explodes a target from within.

- Cauterize: Painfully mends wounded flesh.

- Cease: A universal command to end a hex.

- Chains of Hell: Ensnares a target in burning, razor-edged chains.

- Distance Door: Summons a portal between two points in space.

- Field of Quandric: Covers an area in a dome or sphere of protective force.

- Fissure: Carves a hole in solid material.

- Flames of Tumult: Summons the unstable, infamous energy.

- Flash Flare: Projects an explosive, fiery blast.

- Freezing Flame: Summons eerily chilled fire.

- Frigid Firestorm: Sets forth a rapidly expanding cascade of Freezing Flame.

- Frost Funnel: Projects a cone of icy energy.

- Gale: Projects a powerful jet of air.

- Gigablast: Unleashes a titanic explosion of immense power.

- Grime Glean: Evaporates filth from a recipient.

- Heat Siphon: Draws heat out of a target, cooling it beyond freezing.

- Ice Edge: Coats a blade in ethereal coldness to increase damage inflicted.

- Ignite Illusion: Burns away false images.

- Illuminate: Conjures a glowing orb of light.

- Lava Geyser: Summons a column of molten rock.

- Laser Light: Multiple laser beams conjured from a single source

- Levitate: Lifts objects and people from the ground.

- Lightning Bolts: Summons a tempest of lightning from above.

- Magnetism: Converts etherea into magnetic waves.

- Melt: Liquifies solid material, including rock and metal.

- Mind Chasm: A void-like prison of conscious thought outside the confines of time.

- Other's Blood: A plex hex that imbues the characteristics of a deceased person's blood into the body of another.

- Plasma Aura: Clads a single individual in a second skin of protective force that also burns any who touch its exterior.

- Plasma Spray: Projects a conical jet of white-hot plasma.

- Quandric Cube: A solid manifestation of protective energy, much more durable than a Field of Quandric.

- Realm Gate: Summons a portal between realms.

- Shadow Shift: Grants access to and from the Shade Lands.

- Silence Sphere: Creates a barrier against sounds from outside its borders, and prevents sound from within its borders from escaping.

- Speaking Sphere: Conjures an orb that depicts images of its communicators.

- Spirit Sear: Ignites ectoplasmic matter.

- Tether: Ensnares a target in glowing fibers.

- Thought Link: Creates a conduit between minds for communication.

- Time Hole: Plunges its victim in a sub-dimension outside of temporal reality, where time either accelerates or decelerates.

- Urasik's Ire: A dark plex hex that siphons the life energy of a powerful victim into a mask.

- Volcanic Eruption: Summons a torrent of lava and ash.

- Vigor: Revitalizes a fatigued or unconscious recipient.

- Wind Tunnel: Summons a horizontal, cylindrical vortex.

Technology:

Technology has long since made sizable advances in weaponry. Particle beams, plasma blasts, supersonic magnet guns, etc. are commonplace. As are robots, cybernetics, and heavily armored vehicles. Trojis has a high atmospheric layer called the Xenosphere that randomly annihilates craft that ascend beyond the stratosphere. There is little orbital activity as a result, limiting most three-dimensional travel to the sky. Holographic user interfaces are common, as are data pad personal computers.

Some nations like Crystal Keep and the Union Cities focus mostly on high technology, others like the Holy Alliance are more mancy focused, though they have recently expanded into mechmancy. New Grelland uses all forms of mancy and technology. The Grellish mechmancy sky cits (short for sky citadels) and their tak cannons are among the cornerstones of their defenses.

Nations and Non-State Organizations of Note

- New Grelland: An island nation in the center of the Fire Well on Trojis. The Grells stand against the Holy Alliance in their home realm, and the continued incursions by nether realms within the Fire Well. New Grelland thrives on this adversity. Its martial might is legend throughout the Realms. The Eruption was originally thought to have incinerated the rest of "Old" Grelland, but it still survives in the Pendulum Realm.

- "Old" Grelland: The original nation in West Jeea that came into prominence during the Weird War. Corsis, Bennet Burnhelt, Gathiner, Celsis Kri, Vurg, and many others originally hail from it. It was seemingly incinerated during the events of the Eruption, but Gathiner and Vurg's efforts instead shunted it to the Pendulum Realm.

- Mun'la: A sprawling nation of agricultural communes defended by the Chan'la. A sisterhood of warrior women with space-bending hyper powers, immortality, and peerless martial skills. Mun'la is a close ally of New Grelland, though its role in the Free Jeea Coalition is limited.

- Union Cities: A confederation of three megalopolis city-states. Lan Thedin is the biggest and most significant of them. Kantica is less advanced, but contributes industrial scale. The anarchist haven of Falan, primarily free rides on the other two of its peers, but it contributes psionists and safe passage between Lan Thedin and Kantica's trading routes.

- Crystal Keep: A former fourth member of the Union Cities that seceded centuries earlier. Its advanced technologies make it a formidable world power. The Crystal deep beneath it supplies it with limitless power, which it fanatically guards. It has recently expanded into an exclave in Lantis in an agreement with Decadia.

- Free Jeea Coalition, "FJC": The military partnership of west Jeean nations who are fending off a renewed invasion from the Holy Alliance. The FJC is jointly commanded by New Grelland, Lan Thedin, Kantica, and to a lesser extent, Mun'la.

- Yintu: A secretive aquatic nation sprawling beneath the Holy Alliance. It is home to the dolphin-like Cetari people. Kixie Artis is a member of its ruling class. It does not play a large role in the Game War, but it is referenced on occasion.

- The Holy Alliance: A vast empire lead by Dragons, Titans, and Demons. It takes up the entire eastern half of the Jeean super continent. The Holy Alliance rose soon after the Eruption on Trojis sixteen centuries ago. The Allied Army and Air Navy currently invade the western half of Jeea along the Grym Gulf. Corsis influences it, though its Dragon God, Starm, is unaware of this fact.

- The Horrinshal: The covert wing of the Allied Army focused on intelligence and assassination. It is staffed by Demons and is often on the front lines of any overt or covert military actions of the Holy Alliance.

- The Dirge: An independent guild of smugglers, assassins, and spies who have ties to the Horrinshal through the same dark goddess, Aracna, but the organization is not affiliated with the Holy Alliance and has dealings in Sufrinzon and other Nether Realms. Some of its assassins target Ashe and Avril in the first book. It also works with Hekati in the third book in setting up kliost infection through narcotic sweeteners.

- The Unmaker Laboratory: Hekati's base of operations in the wilds of the Stretch isthmus. The communication and telemetry-jamming rain forests make finding this horrid place a fraught affair. However, it can project its power to places like Mun'la and New Grelland with terrifying ease. It has informal working arrangements with the Holy Alliance, but is independent and often directly supports Corsis's initiatives.

- The Bank of Tromail: The financial arm of the Holy Alliance headed by the tentacled elder god, Tromail, and regional directors like Cartinald Olliday. The financial firm does not see a sustainable path for a long-term conflict with the FJC. It seeks to find a path where peace can be brokered and commerce can flourish.

- Palle: A barony in Sufrinzon's jagged Drand Mountains with Onno as its capital. It quickly conquers all of Alagar and becomes the Palle Empire. It seeks to conquer all of Roaq. Ashe Stelfire and Brigand Company stand in opposition to its ambitions.

- Velsuvia: One of the primary baronies of the Roaq Coalition in Sufrinzon that stand against the rise of Palle. It controls both the island and the Velsuvian Sea in eastern Roaq. Serith, its giant serpent Arch Demon ruler, is honorable but ruthless. He eventually bankrolls the Brigands as an extension of his forces, and often pairs them with the Sharaith marines.

- Darbin: The isthmus barony in eastern Roaq in Sufrinzon that first stands against Palle's rise. Following the defeat of the A Pox, its Darkothe Arch Demon ruler, Baron Urasik, betrays the Roaq Coalition and joins the Palle Empire and ultimately stands victorious as part of Sufrinzon United.

- Necron: A remote island in Sufrinzon's Ocean of the Lost. The death god, Durduun, calls it home. It is his religion's base of operations. No invasion attempts have ever succeeded in taking the island.

- Dread Corps: An army without a nation, arguably the most lethal military force in all the realms. Dread Corpsmen wage war without apparent goals other than to terrorize their adversaries. The organization serves at Corsis's pleasure. They are his means of projecting force when more subtle means fail.

- The Brigands: The mercenary group that fought and lost in the Sufrinzonian War of Reunification. Ashe Stelfire, Welt, and Arwith are former members. The group still exists in a diminished capacity where it hides on the island of Narath in Sufrinzon, but the group does not play a role in the Game War.

- The Bucklers: A group of heroes of which Xax was once a part. They disbanded a few years after Mary Night's death a century ago.

- The Breakers: Xax's name for the gathered team of Players who dare to break the Game's Rules. He also really wanted it to start with a "B".

- The Forever Guard: The legendary Grellish special forces team of immortal warriors commanded directly by the Burnhelt family.

MAJOR RACES

- Humans: The bipedal sentient species dominant in Trojis, Outer Yeom, Inner Yeom, and Pendulum. Due to the ambient etherea in these realms, they live six percent longer than Humans in realms without significant etherea.

  - Long Lived Humans: Primarily of Grellish descent. These are Humans who breathed in the vapors of the dying King of the Weird Ones, but were not in close enough proximity to ascend to godhood. They are blessed and cursed with eternal vitality. They will never die of old age. Only of violence or maladies. They are far less fertile than regular Humans and past on their eternal vitality to their offspring, regardless if one parent is not Long Lived.

- Skin Bots: Androids powered by etherea, exclusively in service to New Grelland. They are treated as Grellish citizens and have the freedom to not serve in Grellish armed forces. Those who abstain can exist freely in the "Playpen" virtual environment. Those who serve in the armed forces are typically in heavy infantry roles, though some engage in technical and espionage professions.

- Chan'la: The order of amazonian warrior women with pointed ears who are Muné's religious order. They defend the weak and stand for justice. The women are also blessed and cursed with eternal vitality. They do not die of old age. Chan'la are either inducted into the order as Humans after an exhaustive vetting process and converted into the new race. Or they are born to existing Chan'la from impregnation in the Divinity Pools, or through sexual coitus with a man. They possess peak of Human strength, speed, and endurance. They also have the innate hyper power of Al'laan that allows them to bend and manipulate space. Chan'la is both singular and plural. They dwell on Trojis and Pendulum.

- Chromatics: An offshoot race of Post Humans who were altered by the etherea of the Eruption. They have brightly colored skin with Onyx (pitch-black), Pale (alabaster-white), Blue, Red, and Green variants. Purple is an especially rare skin tone for them. They are located on Trojis, primarily in the Union Cities and Crystal Keep, where they represent the entire population.

  ○ Suddeners: Genetically synthesized Chromatics who have been fast-grown to adults by Crystal Keep. They are each unique and diverse, rather than identical clones. They have allowed Crystal Keep to massively expand its armed forces in the secret, exclave Lantis base in Decadia. And even more are in Crystal Keep on Trojis.

- Dragons: A vastly powerful race of giant flying reptiles that have multiple shapes and sizes. Some are scaled, others are glossy-smooth, others are feathered. They can shapeshift as small as a Human child. Dragons frequently will assume Human guises to more easily interact with others. They have an innate understanding of mancy. They also are more durable than technological armor and can move in bursts of speed that rival supersonic ships. Dragons also possess a variety of breath attacks like fire, frost, and acid. They are located primarily in Trojis and Inner Yeom.

  ○ Dracoghouls: Dragons that have been resurrected as undead horrors. Unless they are bound to the will of another Dragon, they are dangers to all whom they encounter.

- Murdrakes: Dragonkin hybrids who are born when a Dragon procreates in Human form with another Human. Their skin tones range from Human shades to red, black, green, and blue. They have leathery wings at their back. Some possess vast strength. Others possess enhanced ethereal might. They primarily hail from Trojis and Inner Yeom.

- Titans: Size-changing Post Humans who possess the same immense strength and durability at Human scale, and can reach hundreds of feet tall. They are part of the ruling class in the Holy Alliance, aside from a few notable rebels. They reside primarily in Trojis.

- Sphinxes: Quadrupedal beings of vast ethereal power with Human heads, lion bodies, and eagle wings. They are naturally adept at all forms of mancy and excel at technological and mechmancical engineering. Sphinxes can also assume a bipedal form with dexterous hands, or even apply shapeshifting hexes to appear fully Human. They hail from the Macro Worlds and Inner Yeom.

- Taurus Men: Human-bull hybrids who are all men and all possessing horns and fine fur on their bulky bodies. They are several times stronger than Humans. They dwell in Trojis.

- Weird Ones: Beings of great power composed of Irreality. They must craft shell bodies in order to interact with non-Irreal matter. They all share the Irrealm as their point of origin.

- Cetari: Reclusive, dolphin-like Humanoids who live in the Shallow Sea and the Bottomless Sea in Trojis. Like dolphins, the can hold their breath for long periods and are excellent swimmers. Most of them possess above average strength. But those of royal lineage are many times stronger and more durable than Humans. They reside in Trojis and Inner Yeom.

- Hobgers: Bestial, hulking Post Humans with underbites of sharp teeth. They are honorable and possess great power over desert sands. They are comparatively weaker in non-desert locales. Hobgers primarily live in the Pale Desert on Trojis. They appear mostly in the third and fourth books.

- Draqu: Life-force parasites who can steal their victims' strength, will, memories, and vitality. If they kill their victim, they permanently take their power. They have innate hyper powers to Shadow Shift into the Shade Lands and raise Unnotice auras, allowing them to walk around in plain sight without detection. They reproduce by implanting ectoplasmic larva in their host victim's mind, manifest as sadistic nightmares that torment their host, and then spawn into reality as full-grown Human-like adults when the host looks in a reflective surface, and they step out of it. A nightmare given flesh. They are rare, but often show up in Trojis, Sufrinzon, and Outer Yeom.

- Loknas: Shape-shifting beings comprised of silvery liquid who are immune to much. They often take the form of other beings and can reproduce with them or asexually divide. They can grow in size and manifest blades, new appendages, and virtually any shape they can imagine. Lokna is the singular term for them. They are long lived, but can die from sorrow at the loss of a loved one.

- Redscales: Demons with featherless wings and crimson, scaly hides. They are among the most common Demons. They are stronger than Humans and enjoy eating them. Redscales use technological weapons just as ably as ethereal melee varieties. They hail from all the Nether Realms: Sufrinzon, Decadia. Forboda, among others.

- Almiks: Another common variety of Demons with lanky, but strong hairless bodies and dingy tan-yellow skin. They also use both tech-based and mancy-based weapons. They hail mostly from Sufrinzon and Decadia.

- Mortisis: A common Demon that's an animated skeleton with rust-red bones. Most of them were armor or other clothing. And some of them have enough ethereal mastery in mancy to ascend to positions of authority. They skew more toward ethereal weapons, but they will use tech-based wares on occasion. The singular term for them is Mortisi. They reside primarily in Sufrinzon and Decadia.

- Sokentis: A common Demon with bleeding eye sockets, but they can actually see in 360 degree clarity on all sides. They excel at mancy, combative arts, and can ascend to positions of power. The singular term for them is Sokenti. They hail mainly from Sufrinzon.

- Sharaiths: The black-skinned shark hybrids hailing from Velsuvia in Sufrinzon. They can swim through burning auv or water. They have shark fins topping their heads, jaws of shark teeth, and muscular bodies. Many of them are marines in Velsuvia's armed forces. They're ferocity and competence are renowned in Sufrinzon and in other realms.

- Auvipers: Giant sea serpent Arch Demons that lurk in the burning seas of Sufrinzon. They have glossy black exteriors and can talk without moving their fanged jaws. They also possess vast ethereal command of various forms of mancy. They can also spawn avatars from their flesh in the form of other Demons common to Sufrinzon.

- Nagus Demons: Humanoid Demons with snake tails in place of legs. They have multiple different varieties. Nagus Rattlers have jagged bony rattling mace-like bludgeons on the ends of their tails. Nagus Mambas have oversized jaws with giant fangs. Nagus Cobras have cobra hoods with more comely Human-looking green-skinned faces. Nagus Queens are six-armed longer-tailed variants of Nagus Cobras. They use tech and ethereal-based weapons. They all hail from Forboda.

- Imps: Incredibly fast, toddler sized Demons with small fluttering wings. They excel with blades and also make excellent pilots. They hail from Forboda and Sufrinzon.

- Nymphires: All female, blue-skinned Demons who can Shadow Shift, become invisible, and walk through walls. They are often in assassin or spy professions. They are all converted from other races in a plex hex, and they cannot procreate. They are rare, but tend to show up in Forboda and Trojis.

- Wred Witches: All female, red-skinned Demons with psionic and ethereal mastery. They can both procreate with other beings and induct new members with plex hexes. They reside in Sufrinzon.

- Darkothes: Powerful Arch Demons with dingy-tan, rough skin. They have wings of black fire. They cover their monstrous faces with white, marble-like masks of comely Humans or other races. All of which are molds they took from the corpses of the Human they killed. They can also grow 20 feet tall. Most of them hate Ashe Stelfire on sight because he did the same to one of them with his bronze mask. They live mostly in Sufrinzon.

- Roctalons: Stone winged Demons towering hundreds of feet tall. Denizens of Sufrinzon.

- Skeleborgs: Cyborgs with metal skeletal bones and Human faces. They serve in Decadia.

- Phanos: Demons with orange skin and elegant horns. They reside in Decadia.

- Jethos: Demons composed of green crystalline bodies. They reside in Decadia.

- Cyberions: Nano-tech cyborgs who excel at interfacing with computer systems. They're covered in gold, illuminated, glowing circuitry, and work for Decadia.

- Werewolves: Comparatively rare canine Humanoids who can shape shift from giant, horse-sized wolves to wolf-Human hybrids to regular Human form. They have acute senses of smell, sight, and hearing. They hail from Trojis and Outer Yeom.

- Tarcts: Rocky igneous Humanoid horrors crafted by Hekati on Trojis.

- Pyrae: Stitched together corpses powered by pyromancy. Hekati makes them in Trojis, but others have made them in Sufrinzon.

- Vectras: Flying, aerodynamic cyborgs created by Hekati.

- Tiamanutuls: Immense flying serpents created by Hekati.

- Ultralopod: A gargantuan, squid-horror with trecs-long tentacles that ooze toxic poison. They had been thought extinct in Sufrinzon, but Hekati created a new variety, and others may exist.

- Rune Warriors: Invulnerable warriors with a metallic glaze on their skin covered with glyphs. Corsis is currently the only known being who knows how to create them. They serve Dread Corps.

- Angels: Feather-winged, comely beings who otherwise look like Humans. They have vast strength and durability and can shine potent halo light against their adversaries. Most of them have been slain following the events of the Holy War. Those who survive reside in Trojis, Pendulum, and Sufrinzon.

- Cerulanauts: Six-armed, blue-skinned duelists who were altered from Human form to serve in Dread Corps.

- Titanborgs: Building-sized robotic cyborgs in service of Dread Corps.

- Live Bombs: Human-cyborgs loaded with plasma explosives and a desire to destroy themselves. Used as unnerving first wave weapons by Dread Corps.

- Cykots: Cyborgs with a signal glowing green eye in the center of their heads. They serve in Dread Corps.

GLOSSARY

- **A Pox**: A sentient, malicious disease that manifests in pitch black sores.

- **Adapting Blade**: A weapon filled with nano machines that imbue its user with varying powers depending on the need.

- **Aesur** (A-Surr): An abomination of pulsing grey flesh that can grow multiple limbs. It absorbs people into its pachyderm-sized form. They become Aesur Riders while fused to the body, or Aesur Rovers when moving outside the body, attached to ectoplasmic tentacles. It is related to the larger Usur. The monstrosity serves Dread Corps.

- **Al'laan** (All-Awn): The mental manipulation of space. Related to psionic energy and etherea.

- **Alagar** (Al-Ah-Gar): The eastern portion of the Rouq-Alagar super continent in Sufrinzon. The baronies of Palle, Harac, Tartus, Eurphi, Carnist, East Nrith and Barithania are counted among its nations.

- **Almik**: A lanky, tan-skinned Demon.

- **Alterv Gun**: A legendary revolver that fires corrosive, burning bullets.

- **Aracna** (Ar-Ack-Nah): A six-armed Demon goddess of murder who allied herself to Starm during the Holy War on Trojis. She later founded the Dirge.

- **Arch Demon**: A general term used to describe the most powerful members of the Demonic races. Some are born into the position, others earn it.

- **Archmancer**: A mancer with supreme prowess in a vast number of ethereal disciplines.

- **Arielle** (Air-E-El): A finger-sized servant of Halonir.

- **Arwith** (Are-With): A Psyspecter with considerable psionic might. His misty body has no substance. A member of Brigand Company.

- **Ashe Stelfire** (Aesh Stell-Fire): An arrogant pyromancer who must become someone better or someone worse after crossing paths with Corsis. Father of Avril Enzali. Alias: Repenter.

- **Aura of Quandric** (Kwan-Drik): Named for the Dragon who invented the hex. A transparent cloak of protective energy that can be fortified with other hexes. The aura clings to a single person like a second skin.

- **Auv**: Corrosive, fiery liquid that comprises the majority of Sufrinzon's oceans and rivers.

- **Avril Enzali** (Av-Ril En-Zall-E): A determined woman raised as a Krian warrior by her surrogate father, Eric. She is the biological daughter of Baroness Nom'Iniv and Ashe Stelfire.

- **Bander of Whitewood**: A amicable Werewolf whose savage fighting style belies his gentle heart. He is a citizen of New Grelland. A member of the Forever Guard.

- **Barithania** (Barr-Ih-Thane-Ee-Ah): A hellish expanse of hardpan desert and deep canyons. Fire burns within the cracks of the barony's earth.

- **Baronies**: A Nation-state within Sufrinzon. All the baronies were once united under Empress Menusa's empire before the Grells defeated them.

- **Baslak**: A broad-bladed sword with serrated edges.

- **Battle Marshal**: A position of highest military authority. The title is used by both Grells and Krians.

- **Bennet Burnhelt**: The leader of New Grelland. Father to Vick Burnhelt. He has a long history with Corsis. Alias: Benefactor.

- **Biers**: A Jymoth chief of Zirh.

- **Bi-Month**: A period of time measuring just over sixty days, or a sixth of a Trojisi year.

- **Bleed**: A dagger that causes all of its victim's blood to gush out its stab wound.

- **Blite**: The second bi-month of the Trojisi year.

- **Brigand Company**: A force of approximately two hundred soldiers under Gnorok's command. They are the heroes of the Rouq Coalition. Its other members of note include Repenter, ViRauni, Frulgrath, Salatha, Welt, Thebes, Tin Skin and Arwith.

- **Bucklers**: The infamous group of Trojisi adventurers who disbanded decades earlier. Jovel Wrenrot, Vance Vulcan, Xax and Marilyn the Greater are their known members.

- **Carnist** (Carr-Nist): A region of rolling hills and dormant forests. Grass grows over ancient ruins of what was once the mightiest barony in Sufrinzon, grandeur lost in the haze of time.

- **Celsis Kri** (Sell-Siss Cry) A goddess of conquest who fought on the side of Starm before the Eruption on Trojis. The Dragon God betrayed her. She has been imprisoned for sixteen centuries.

- **Chan'la** (Shawn-Lah): Warrior women hailing from Northern Jeea, known for their pointed ears and mastery of Al'laan.

- **Charlemagnus** (Char-La-Magg-Nuss): The deceased father of Sol-neena and husband of Ramansa. The Sphinx was killed by Baron Jonas.

- **Chronomancy**: The practice of manipulating time and space with etherea.

- **Cinder**: A red dagger that injects fire through anything it stabs.

- **Clatch**: A glassy staff of immense ethereal might.

- **Claudia**: A female Dire Wolf.

- **Clote Narn**: A Demon without skin on its exposed muscles.

- **Colco** (Coll-Co): A succulent poultry bird.

- **Colossus**: A building-sized suit of bulky, hollow armor created by Dread Corps.

- **Corsis** (Core-Siss): A reptilian archmancer who craves entertainment. He keeps out of the public eye. Alias: The Lizard.

- **Cosm**: The Pico Realm that is the urban hub of the Underguild.

- **Darbin** (Dar-Binn): The Sufrinzon barony comprised of tundra and mountains. Its isthmus connects Rouq to Alagar.

- **Darkothe** (Dar-Kothe): An Arch Demon with flaming black wings and leathery skin with power equal to that of a Dragon. They often wear white masks molded after comely Humans.

- **Dead Straits**: The narrow channel between East and West Nrith. It connects the Kalcan Ocean to the Velsuvian Sea.

- **Demon**: A sentient being given to evil. They hail from Nether Realms. They sometimes call themselves Nether Children.

- **Deva Falc** (Deh-Vah Falk): The Baroness of Barithania.

- **Dhalia** (Dal-Ee-Ah): Durduun's personal assassin and younger sister. Alias: Doom Girl.

- **Dire Wolves**: A team of undead Werewolves who serve the Dirge.

- **Dirge**: An organization of assassins that inflicts harm in dozens of realms.

- **Distance Door**: An ethereal portal that bends space within a realm to bridge the distance between two locations, regardless of proximity.

- **Doom Girls**: Durduun's nickname for his two sisters, Dhalia and Suso. They serve him as assassins.

- **Door Spider**: A Human-sized, Demonic spider with the innate ability to create Distance Doors.

- **Double Shot**: A breach-loaded pistol capable of inflicting great damage with its ethereally charged bullets. The weapon can only fire twice before reloading.

- **Dragons**: Immensely potent creatures of great ethereal sophistication. They typically take on the forms of reptilian, winged giants, however they often take on other guises.

- **Drand Mountains**: A cyclopean mountain range in Sufrinzon. They are said to be the tallest mountains in the known realms. Clouds perpetually cover their zenith.

- **Drandfiev** (Drand-Feev): The imperial vestments worn by Empress Menusa.

- **Dread Corps** (Dred Core): A sadistic army without a nation that operates across many realms.

- **Dread Doors**: Realm Gates used by Dread Corps, noted by their glowing red borders and pointed arches.

- **Drimithu** (Drim-Ih-Thu): An obscure martial art incorporating the use of battle axes in its fighting style.

- **Dukalc** (Dew-Kallc): A barony of Sufrinzon in northern Rouq filled with fiery deserts of black sand in the north and tangled forests in the south.

- **Durduun** (Durr-Dune): The pale-skinned God of Death. Brother of Suso and Dhalia, whom he calls the Doom Girls. He knows ViRauni well.

- **East Nrith** (Nrehth): A mostly unpopulated barony in Sufrinzon with dense jungles on the Alagar side of the Dead Straits. Rivers and lakes of corrosive cauv crisscross its landscape.

- **Een of Muné** (Een of Moon-A): A Chan'la warrior woman who is also closely allied to the Grells. A member of the Forever Guard.

- **Eric Enzali** (Er-Ik En-Zall-E): The leader of the Krians for the past sixteen centuries. He adopted Avril at the behest of Svithe. Alias: Battle Marshall (rank).

- **Eruption**: The cataclysm that killed nations and birthed others. It is the zero point of the Trojisi calander, which is used in other realms including Sufrinzon.

- **Etherea** (E-Ther-E-Ah): A powerful energy source outside of the electromagnetic spectrum that powers all forms of mancy.

- **Ethereal Spectrum**: The range of all possible frequencies of etherea.

- **Eurphi** (Yur-Fi): An atypical place of beauty within Sufrinzon. The barony is famous for its arts, even in other realms.

- **Falan** (Fal-Ahn): A city-state in Jeea renowned for its anarchist community.

- **Fear's Flight**: A flying, monolithic creature with countless tentacles.

- **Fiber Armor**: Protective garb comprised of carbon-reinforced fibers renowned for both durability and flexibility.

- **Field of Quandric** (Kwan-Drik): Named for the Dragon who created the hex. A transparent dome of protective energy that can be fortified with other hexes. The field can encompass large amounts of space.

- **Fire Well**: A sea of ethereal Flames of Tumult contained by the Outer Wall on Trojis. It burns on the remains of Old Grelland.

- **Flames of Tumult** (Tuh-Mult): Violently powerful flames that can incinerate most anything. They move like lightning.

- **Fleshmancy**: The ethereal practice of horribly transforming living creatures into new beings.

- **Flynn Fellen** (Flinn Fell-Enn): The venerable champion of the Grells who wields the warhammer, Kark's Fist. He has more combat experience than anyone on Trojis. A member of the Forever Guard.

- **Forever Guard**: The elite military unit of undying defenders of New Grelland. Een of Muné, Bander of Whitewood, Flynn Fellen, Kindra Shalai and Vick Burnhelt make up its members.

- **Frivon Ice**: Frozen ethereal matter that cannot easily be melted or broken. It is far stronger than steel.

- **Frulgrath** (Frule-Grath): A gaunt, four-armed Demon with dried skin. A member of Brigand Company. Alias: Hatchet Man.

- **Garland**: The Rune Warrior bodyguard of Corsis.

- **Garret Parvenplath**: The second-in-command of the Krians.

- **Gaun Herb**: A rare and coveted plant that vastly slows the aging process of those who smoke it. One puff is said to elongate its user's life span by a decade.

- **Gathiner**: The Olden God of Invention.

- **Geomancy**: The practice of creating stone and earth based hexes.

- **Ghalmenq** (Gal-Menk): A frigid Icilith Demoness with ties to Vi-Rauni.

- **Ginj** (Ginge): The animated dead woman chained to the mast of the Ginj Crier. She is the source of its propulsion.

- **Ginj Crier** (Ginge-Cry-Err): The wooden sailing ship commanded by Captain Heelinu.

- **Gnorok** (Nor-Ock): A skilled Murdrake mercenary. He wears scarves over his head to hide his bearded face. He leads Brigand Company. Alias: Gnor.

- **Gorgul** (Gore-Gull): Grey-skinned psionic members of Dread Corps with eye-tipped tentacles growing from their heads.

- **Greater Demon**: A general term used to describe the more powerful members of the Demonic races. Some are born into the position, others earn it.

- **Grell**: A person hailing from Old Grelland or New Grelland.

- **Grellish Claw**: The three pronged insignia of the Grells.

- **Gunbug**: A flying assault vehicle of Grellish design.

- **Gunmancer**: A mancer who infuses etherea into guns, a specialized type of mechmancer.

- **Halbask**: A pole arm with a slender, curving blade along half its length.

- **Halonir** (Hal-Oh-Neer): A sentient forest located in Inner Yeom. It is capable of acting through trees in any other realm.

- **Halonir's Sap** (Hal-Oh-Neers Sapp): Curative, sweet syrup secreted by the largest tree in Halonir.

- **Hans Achillius** (Hons Ah-Kill-E-Uss): A robotic Grellish doctor.

- **Harac** (Har-Rak): A mountainous barony of Sufrinzon in southern Alagar.

- **Harcruazeder** (Har-Cru-Ah-Zedd-Urr): An Arch Roctalon with ties to ViRauni.

- **Heelinu** (Hee-Lin-Ew): The Almik captain of the Ginj Crier.

- **Hekati** (Heh-Kot-E): A goddess of knowledge who allied herself to Starm during the Holy War on Trojis. She is on good terms with the Holy Alliance and the baronies of Sufrinzon. She is a master of many ethereal arts such as fleshmancy and mechmancy.

- **Hex**: An application of etherea directed by a mancer for a specific effect. Most often a hex requires a mancer to align his or her inner physiology through hand gestures followed by a command word or phrase.

- **Hexember** (Hex-Emm-Berr): The sixth bi-month of the Trojisi year.

- **Holkstill** (Holc-Stil): A Greater Demon in the form of a giant, reptilian eye wreathed with thorny tentacles.

- **Holy Alliance**: An inaptly-named empire controlled by powerful despots on Jeea in Trojis.

- **Holy War**: The Trojisi conflict that led to the Eruption.

- **Hook**: ViRauni's zweihaender sword named for the second hook-shaped blade on the bottom of its hilt.

- **Horace**: A Satyr general of the Rouq Coalition in Darbin. He is an old ally of Gnorok.

- **Hrolish** (Hrawl-Ish): An arcane, ethereal language that unmakes anything its speaker desires.

- **Hydromancy**: The practice of creating ice and water based hexes.

- **Icilith** (Ice-Ill-Ith): A greater Demon made of durable ice.

- **Imp**: A toddler-sized Demon who moves at great speeds on fluttering under-sized wings.

- **Info Company**: A nationless media organization on Trojis dealing in both news and entertainment.

- **Inner Yeom** (Yee-Ohm): A verdant realm of primeval nature. Halonir resides within its borders.

- **Inparadis**: Starm's private pico realm.

- **IRM**: Short for inter realm messenger. A device created by Ramansa to relay recorded messages from one realm to another.

- **Iron Spitter**: The standard issue long arm of the forces of Sufrinzon, renowned for its ability to pierce armor and hard flesh.

- **Irrealm** (Ear-Relm): The place between the cracks of space and time.

- **Janey Appleton**: A Krian who trained Avril Enzali during her childhood.

- **Jarah**: The first woman to wear the ViRauni armor.

- **Jasphir Iniv** (Jas-Fer In-Ivv): The Sokenti outcast of the Iniv family who allies himself to Ashe Stelfire. He specializes in knives. Alias: Jas.

- **Jeea** (Jee-Ah): The sprawling super-continent that comprises the majority of Trojis' land. New Grelland and the Holy Alliance occupy opposite ends of it.

- **Jeean** (Jee-An): 1) Of or pertaining to Jeea. 2) The trade language spoken throughout Trojis.

- **Jymoth** (Jy-Moth): A Furry, humanoid, moth-like Arch Demon.

- **Jonas**: The Baron of Wrilock. His armor conceals his true form. He has run afoul of Ashe Stelfire, Gnorok, Ramansa and Solneena in the past.

- **Jovel Wrenrot** (Joe-Vell Renn-Rott): The legendary, Trojisi swordsman without a nation.

- **Kalcan Ocean** (Cal-Cann): The vast body of auv to the north of the Rouq-Alagar super continent in Sufrinzon.

- **Kali** (Cal-E): The Baroness of Harac.

- **Kindra Shalai** (Kinn-Drah Shah-Ly): A fierce champion of New Grelland. Wife to Vick Burnhelt. A member of the Forever Guard.

- **Klavensol** (Klave-En-Saul): A sword with a slightly curved, slender blade. It can be easily wielded in one hand or two.

- **Klifer** (Kly-Ferr): A Redscale sailor serving on the Ginj Crier

- **Klon**: The Darkothe heir of Darbin. Son of Lilith and Urasik.

- **Krakaus** (Crack-Awes): The last surviving Lord of Sufrinzon who dwells in the Ocean of the Lost.

- **Kraumaph** (Krow-Maff): Undead giants suspended by airborne chains like marionettes.

- **Kri Enclave**: The Krians' secluded base of operations in northern Jeea.

- **Krian** (Cry-Ann): The sect of warriors who follow the mantra of Celsis Kri the Conqueror.

- **Lara Birkin**: A female Krian warrior.

- **Light of Nuul** (Nule): Pitch black energy that consumes anything it touches, including the very air.

- **Lightning Gunner**: A Grellish soldier with an apparatus that projects surges of electricity.

- **Liloth**: The Darkothe Baroness of Darbin. Wife to Baron Urasik.

- **Loci Ocean** (Low-Sy): The sea of Auv that burns to the west of the Rouq-Alagar super continent.

- **Lokna** (Lock-Nah): A creature of liquid metal that shape-shifts into solid forms.

- **Lornes River** (Lornz Riv-Err): The channel of auv flowing through Narth.

- **Macro Worlds**: A network of fifty-five planets all sharing a nebula-sized atmosphere of oxygen, nitrogen and carbon dioxide. They are now desolate following the first A Pox pandemic.

- **Mancer**: A well-studied person who controls etherea for a multitude of uses.

- **Mancy**: The study and/or application of etherea.

- **Manx**: A female animated skeleton, not related to Mortisis. She serves on the Ginj Crier.

- **Marilyn the Greater**: An enigmatic angel who fought at Jovel Wrenrot's side. A member of the Bucklers.

- **Martialmancer** (Mar-Shall-Manse-Err): A mancer who specializes in combative uses of etherea.

- **Mechmancer** (Mek-Manse-Err): A mancer who infuses etherea into machines.

- **Menusa** (Men-Ew-Sah): The Empress of Sufrinzon who was slain centuries earlier.

- **Microwave Blaster**: A weapon that fires concentrated microwaves.

- **Mol Granz**: The forgotten Queen of the Grells. Alias: ViRauni.

- **Mortisi** (More-Tiss- E): Demonic, animated skeletons who speak without moving their jaws.

- **Moth's Port**: The capital of Zirh, a strategic shipping and naval city for Rouq.

- **Murdrake**: A hybrid of a Human and a Dragon.

- **Narath**: A remote island somewhere in the Ocean of the Lost. It is home to both Ashe Stelfire and ViRauni.

- **Necromancer**: A mancer specializing in death.

- **Necron**: The secluded island of Durduun's temple, hidden within the Ocean of the Lost.

- **Nero**: The smallest of the Dire Wolves.

- **Nether Children**: An honorific for Demons.

- **Nether Realm**: A secluded sphere of existence tainted by evil and peopled by the damned.

- **New Grelland**: Formerly named Haven Isle, it survives in the center of the Fire Well. Its people continue to honor Old Grelland's heroic legacy.

- **Nirva Iniv** (Ner-va In-Ivv): The Human Baroness of Palle. She married into the Iniv family to amass political and arcane might. Mother of Arvil Enzali. Alias: Nirva Silv.

- **Nixer** (Nix-Err): A klavensol sword originally used by Eric Enzali. Its potent Harm Hex inflicts damage on its victims that cannot be healed.

- **Nunaker** (Noon-Nack-Err): A Lokna ally to Ashe Stelfire.

- **Nuul Sphere** (Nule Sphere): An expanding circle of pitch black light that annihilates anything it touches. Alias: Rid Reaction.

- **Nuul Wand** (Nule Wand): A device that projects Light of Nuul with a finite number of charges.

- **Olden Gods**: Deities who held sway over Trojis and Sufrinzon before the Eruption.

- **Ocean of the Lost**: The burning sea of auv in Sufrinzon that meddles with all navigation as one moves farther into its vast expanse.

- **Octavian** (Oct-A-Vee-Enn): The leader of the Dire Wolves.

- **Old Grelland**: A nation of thinkers and heroes. It was annihilated in the Eruption on Trojis.

- **Omsteel** (Ohm-Steel): Glossy, hard-carbon material that looks like steel, though considerably more durable.

- **One Shot**: A breach-loaded pistol capable of inflicting great damage with its ethereally charged bullets. The weapon can only fire once before reloading.

- **Onno** (Awn-O): The capital of Palle. It is hidden at the top of the Drand Mountains and unreachable through the miasma shrouding their peaks.

- **Outer Yeom** (Yee-Ohm): A ravaged realm where everyone knows Corsis's name.

- **Palle Empire** (Pawl): The baronies conquered or annexed by Palle in Alagar. It seeks to expand through all of Sufrinzon.

- **Palle** (Pawl): A mountainous barony in the heart of the Drand Mountains. Its leadership seeks to conquer all of Sufrinzon.

- **Panic Room**: A pico realm created by Ramansa to serve as a sanctuary from attackers.

- **Particle Beam**: An energy beam containing solid specks of matter.

- **Pendulum**: A mysterious Pico Realm known by very few.

- **Perceptia**: A sixth sense attuned to spiritual phenomena.

- **Pico Realm**: A plane of existence with limited space and finite borders.

- **Pirix**: A finger-sized humanoid with feathered, fluttering wings.

- **Planet Realm**: A sphere of existence that orbits a daystar. Its people are both good and evil.

- **Plasma**: The white hot fourth state of matter.

- **Plex Hex**: Short for Complex Hex. An application of larger amounts of etherea that typically requires greater preparation by one or more mancers for a specific effect.

- **Portal Projector**: A wide barreled gun created by gunmancy. It creates rounded Distance Doors and Charred Doors.

- **Psionic Energy** (Sy-Onn-Ick): A force of the mind intertwined with the electromagnetic and ethereal spectrums.

- **Psyspecter** (Sy-Spec-Terr): A spectral mind without a body.

- **Punch Round**: A bullet for the One Shot or Double Shot that is said to punch through anything.

- **Pyrae** (Py- Ray): Reanimated corpses implanted with Demonic organs within stitched wounds. Fire burns upon them without consuming their durable flesh.

- **Pyrene** (Py-Reen): The first bi-month of the Trojisi year.

- **Pyromancer** (Py-Row-Manse-Err): A mancer specializing in fire-based hexes.

- **Quandric** (Kwan-Drik): An infamous Dragon who did not converge on Trojis with the rest of his kin. He is not affiliated with the Holy Alliance.

- **Quar Iniv** (Kwar In-Ivv): The Sokenti Baron of Palle. He seeks to conquer all of Sufrinzon.

- **Quatres** (Kwat-Rez): The fourth bi-month of the Trojisi year.

- **Quintember** (Quinn-Temm-Berr): The fifth bi-month of the Trojisi year.

- **Quoth** (Kwoth): The mother of Gnorok.

- **Ramansa** (Ram-ahn-zah): A powerful Sphinx who owes Ashe Stelfire a favor. She is a member of the Underguild and mother to Solneena. Alias: Rammy.

- **Realm Gate**: An ethereal portal with burning edges that bridges two realms to one another.

- **Realm of Thought**: An immaterial sphere of reality only accessible by the mind and soul.

- **Realm**: A sphere or plane of reality.

- **Redscale**: The most common Demonic race named for their blood-hued, scaly skin. They fly with leathery wings.

- **Repenter** (Ree-Pent-Err): A masked member of Brigand Company. Alias: Ashe Stelfire.

- **Retributor** (Ree-Tri-Bute-Ore): The legendary Adapting Blade once wielded by Bennet Burnhelt in an age long gone. The double-bladed, battle axe fell into Corsis' possession some time later.

- **Ricardo Alterv**: A gun-wielding ally to Ashe Stelfire. Alias: Rico.

- **Rip**: A skeletal servant of Durduun, unrelated to Mortisis.

- **Rithic** (Rith-Ick): Ashe Stelfire's Darkothe mentor who died at his protege's hands. Ashe infused his life energy in a bronze mask molded in the likeness of his Demonic face.

- **Roctalon** (Rock-Tal-Onn): Size-changing Greater Demons made of stone. Fire blazes within them.

- **Romulus** (Rom-U-Luss): A male Dire Wolf.

- **Rouq** (Roke): The western portion of the Rouq-Alagar super continent in Sufrinzon. The baronies of Darbin, Urkalc, Dukalc, Wrilock, Sulph, Zirh, Velsuvia and West Nrith are counted among its nations.

- **Rouq Coalition** (Roke Co-Al-Lish-On): A military alliance between the baronies of Rouq dedicated to the preservation of their independence from the Palle Empire.

- **Run River**: The burning border between Carnist and Barthania.

- **Rune Warriors**: Indestructible men and women glazed in polished metal. Sinuous runes twine over their bodies like elaborate tattoos.

- **Salamen** (Sall-Ah-Menn): Amphibious, four-armed Demons who thrive in the buring auv.

- **Salatha** (Sall-Ah-Thah): A Wred Witch who allies herself to the Rouq Coalition. A member of Brigand Company.

- **Satyr** (Say-Turr): A Demon with cloven feet and pointed horns.

- **Selphi** (Sel-Fee): A mancer employed by Ramansa.

- **Serith** (Serr-Ith): The Baron of Velsuvia. A trustworthy Auviper of honor and staunch supporter of Brigand Company.

- **Seska**: The female, subordinate Rune Warrior in service of Dread Corps.

- **Shade Lands:** A realm of compressed space accessible by shadows. It serves as a shortcut over long distances for those brave enough to tread through its twilit expanse.

- **Sokenti** (So-Ken-Tee): A comely, Demonic race without eyes. Blood perpetually ebbs from their empty sockets.

- **Solneena** (Sole-Nee-Nah): An inquisitive Sphinx with an affinity for face piercings. She is the daughter of Ramansa. Alias: Neena.

- **Spatial Sheath**: A pocket of compressed space capable of storing vast amounts of mass without hindrance to person carrying it. It is often attached to articles of clothing or armor.

- **Sphere Round**: A bullet for the One Shot or Double Shot that creates a cascading, spherical explosion.

- **Sphinx**: A powerful, intelligent creature with the wings of an eagle, the body of a lion and the head of Human.

- **Stage**: The perpetual, three-dimensional vantage point displaying Ashe Stelfire to Avril Enzali.

- **Starm**: A Dragon God who controls the Holy Alliance.

- **Stretch**: A treacherous isthmus in northern Jeea on Trojis.

- **Striving Gods**: A group of Olden Gods who fought against Old Grelland in the Holy War.

- **Sufrinzon** (Suff-Rihn-Zahn): A Nether Realm beset with perpetual dark clouds and endless strife. It is a twisted reflection of Trojis.

- **Sulph** (Sulf): An island barony in Sufrinzon's mapped portion of the Ocean of the Lost. Marshlands cover it.

- **Suso** (Suze-O): Durduun's personal assassin and youngest sister. Alias: Doom Girl.

- **Svithe**: (Svythe): A peddler of all things rare. Bandages cover his entire body due to alleged burn related injuries.

- **Tak Cannon**: A vastly powerful energy weapon used by both New Grelland and Dread Corps.

- **Tartan Mortisi** (Tar-Tann More-Tiss-Ee): Muscle-bound Demons hailing from the frozen barony of Tartus. No flesh covers their skulls.

- **Tartan Ocean** (Tar-Tann): The western body of auv to the east of the Rouq-Alagar super continent in Sufrinzon.

- **Tartus**: An icy barony located in northeast Alagar in Sufrinzon.

- **Tempes** (Temp-Ees): A jaundiced commander of Dread Corps who uses chronomancy.

- **Temple Tavomine** (Tav-Oh-Mine): The secluded headquarters of Starm's closest followers in the Holy Alliance.

- **Thebes** (Theebs): A rambunctious Imp with a great talent for reconnaissance. A member of Brigand Company.

- **Tin Skin**: A cyborg covered in a deceptively-durable, tin-like chassis. A member of Brigand Company. Alias: Tinny.

- **Tonnin's Fork** (Tah-Ninns Fork): A tuning fork that generates an extremely loud, disorienting toll.

- **Tower Stelfire** (Stell-Fire): The isolated home of Ashe Stelfire on in western Narath.

- **Trec**: A standard unit of measurement for distance. Five-thousand feet equals one trec.

- **Trires** (Try-Rez): The third bi-month of the Trojisi year.

- **Trojis** (Troj-Iss): The planet realm with a troubled past, present and future. It orbits the daystar.

- **Trojisi** (Troj-Iss-E): Something or someone originating from Trojis.

- **Tromail** (Tro-Male): A formless, tentacle-covered god of evil who allied itself to Starm during the Holy War on Trojis. Greatly diminished from its former might, it is the last of the elder gods who fell in an age long past.

- **Tsaus** (Saus): A necromancer serving Durduun.

- **Tyborg**: Thirty-foot tall cyborgs created by Dread Corps.

- **Underguild**: An organization of mancers that pools its resources to refine and enhance all ethereal arts. It also deals in darker aspects of the unknown.

- **Urasik** (Ur-Ah-Sick): The Darkothe Baron of Darbin. Husband to Baroness Lilith and father to Klon. Creater of the "Urasik's Ire" plex hex, which siphons the life energy of a powerful victim into a mask.

- **Urkalc** (Urr-Kallc): A barony of Sufrinzon in western Rouq filled with fiery deserts of black sand. It is the home of the Loci Bank.

- **Usur** (Oo-Surr): A building-sized creature of pulsing grey flesh. Like the smaller Aesur, it grows multiple limbs and absorbs people into its form. They become Usur Riders while fused to the body, or Usur Rovers when moving outside the body, attached to ectoplasmic tentacles. The monstrosity serves Dread Corps.

- **Vamberg**: A straight-edged sword with a slender blade. It can only be wielded in one hand.

- **Vance Vulcan**: A size-changing grenadier possessing gargantuan strength and durability. A member of the Bucklers.

- **Velsuvia** (Vell-Su-Vee-Ah): A powerful barony of islands within the

Velsuvian Sea in Sufrinzon. Its Demonic people are typified by their fierce martial tradition.

- **Vick Burnhelt**: The son of Bennet Burnhelt. Husband to Kindra Shalai. The mechmancer saved New Grelland from the fires of the Eruption. A member of the Forever Guard.

- **Victim Zero**: The disheveled first host of the A Pox.

- **ViRauni** (Vy-Ronn-E): A haunted woman in cursed red armor. A member of Brigand Company. Alias: Mol Granz.

- **ViRauni's Forest** (Vy-Ronn-Ees): A sickly forest on the eastern side of Narath.

- **War of No Hope**: The decades long siege of Dread Corps on Jeea.

- **Welt**: A headless gunmancer with ties to Ramansa, Durduun and the Underguild. A member of Brigand Company.

- **West Nrith** (Nrehth): A mostly unpopulated barony in Sufrinzon with dense jungles on the Roaq side of the Dead Straits. Rivers and lakes of corrosive cauv crisscross its landscape.

- **Wred Witch** (Red Witch): A Demonic female mancer skilled in both psionic and ethereal disciplines.

- **Wrilock** (Rill-Ock): A mountainous barony in western Rouq with treacherous woodlands and plains.

- **Xax** (Zaks): A grinning, seven-foot tall robot who roves the realms to protect those who can't protect themselves. A member of the Bucklers.

- **Xeno** (Zee-No): A wavelength of the ethereal spectrum that reveals non-corporeal phenomena not perceptible on the electromagnetic spectrum.

- **Yars**: The male, commanding Rune Warrior in service of Dread Corps.

- **Zandris** (Zand-Riss): The capital city of Old Grelland.

- **Zirh** (Zur): An island barony in Sufrinzon in a mapped area of the Ocean of the Lost.

- **Zweihaender** (Zwy-Hand-Ur): A two-handed great sword.

AFTERWORD

I hope you enjoyed Repenter: The Hidden Chapters. Ashe, Avril, and the rest of their allies still have trecs to go. Nirva and Quar Iniv still rule the East. They all Play the Game. All to the delight of Corsis. The story continues in Players of the Game Book 2: The Brigands. Available now.

Please also submit a review on your retailer or review site of choice. It helps other readers like you find this story.

Join the James McGowan Reader Group at stelfire.com to get notified of all new releases in the series.

ABOUT THE AUTHOR

James McGowan lives in Nebraska. In addition to writing, he enjoys enticing his lovely wife with new recipes, though his black bean Marsala pasta is a favorite standby. While writing is his passion, he also likes getting out of the house for walks and hikes. He's always up for a game of pitch with friends too. James is a fan of comic books and often enjoys their adaptations to other media. He's a member of the Nebraska Writers Workshop, the Nebraska Writers Guild, and the Alliance of Independent Authors.

Website: stelfire.com

Facebook Fan Page: JamesMcGowanAuthor

Join the James McGowan Reader Group at stelfire.com

Get a notification email for all new releases in the series at https://books2r ead.com/author/james-mcgowan/subscribe/1/174474/